FIGHTER'S FAKE OUT

A. RIVERS

1

———————

Jimmy

The moment I step outside the MMA gym where I train as a professional fighter, I hear someone talking. I'm sweating like crazy from the workout my coach put me through, and my heart is pounding in my ears, but I recognize the voice.

Enya.

I could probably be blindfolded underwater and still know Enya's voice when I hear it. I had a crush on the woman long before I ever met her, but since we started training together, my feelings have spiraled out of control. Not that she knows I exist, except as some kind of younger brother figure. Because that's just my fucking luck.

But I've never heard her like this. She sounds stressed. Unhappy. I hesitate by the corner of the building, not wanting to interrupt. Unfortunately, she's standing between me and my car, which is parked in the lot adjoining Crown MMA—the premier facility for training professional MMA fighters in Las Vegas.

"Please don't," she begs. "The last thing I need is to spend the weekend of Emma's wedding trying to juggle five blind dates just so you guys can settle a bet. You know how much I hate when you set me up."

My jaw firms. This again. Enya previously mentioned her sister is trying to arrange a blind date for when she visits Wisconsin. The idea of her spending time with one man is bad enough, but five? If I have to sit on the sidelines while that happens, I'll go fucking insane.

"I don't care if you think your guy is perfect for me. I'm asking you to drop this and make sure the others do too."

I wince. If there's anything I hate, it's Enya being distressed. I've been mulling over her blind date situation since she first told me about it. Maybe it's time to man up and do something about my crush. I can't continue this way forever.

Straightening my shoulders, I round the corner and find Enya with one hand on her hip, the other pressing a phone to her ear. My insides tremble, but I march up to her and hold out a hand. "Give me the phone."

She shakes her head and tries to wave me away.

"Please," I persist.

She cocks her head. "Hang on a sec, Kels."

She passes me the phone.

I raise it to my ear. "Enya will call you back in a moment."

Then I hang up.

Enya's mouth drops open. "What the hell?" she demands. "That was my sister!"

"I don't care who it was. She was upsetting you."

"So you hung up on her?" She jabs me in the chest with a finger. "You can't just do that."

I try to ignore the angry flash of her gorgeous brown eyes and the adorable tilt of her upturned nose. If I let myself stare at her, I'll forget what I want to say, and that will get me nowhere fast. "You need a date for your sister's wedding."

She rolls her eyes. "It seems I already have five of them. Have you decided to get on the bandwagon and set me up with one of your friends too?"

"God no." I shudder at the thought. "I'm offering myself as an alternative. Tell Kelsey that you can't do any blind dates because you're already bringing someone. *Me.*"

For a long moment, she doesn't respond and I think she's considering the possibility. But then she laughs. Fucking *laughs*. Discomfort prickles across my skin, but I don't rescind the offer. I've finally grown a set of balls, and I refuse to back down.

"You can't seriously want to spend an entire weekend with my crazy family just to save me from the awkwardness of a few blind dates."

I relax, relieved her laughter has nothing to do with me. I already know she's a million miles out of my league, and I'd been scared she might tell me so to my face. Not that she's cruel enough to do that, but fear isn't always logical. I cross my arms and give her a look. "Can and do. It's win-win. You get to avoid a fuckton of awkwardness and I get a trip to Wisconsin."

She scoffs. "Yeah, because Wisconsin is everybody's idea of a great holiday destination."

I shrug. "Could be worse. I've never been before."

In fact, I've never been out of Nevada, but I don't feel like admitting that. She's competed in Europe, Australia, and the United Kingdom. Compared to her, I've led a very sheltered life.

"You know my family live on a farm, right?" She sounds skeptical. "And they're crazy. Did I mention that part already?"

The grin I'm trying to hide surfaces. "You did."

She frowns. "You want to spend a weekend on a farm in Wisconsin with a bunch of people you don't know who will interrogate you mercilessly?"

As long as I'm with her, I'll happily do anything. But if I tell her that, she'll freak out. So I give her the simple answer. "Yep. That's right. Glad you understand."

She searches my gaze, and I think she might turn me down, but then she gives a faint nod and holds out a hand. "Can I have my phone back?"

ENYA

I'm tempted to take Jimmy up on his offer. It would save me a lot of awkwardness. I'm *very* tempted. But as he lays my phone on my palm, I don't immediately call Kelsey to let her know the news. Instead, I decide to give him one last chance to change his mind.

"It's sweet of you to offer, but I don't think you know what you're getting yourself into. You'll regret your decision about two-point-five seconds after you arrive, and by then it will be too late to escape."

He doesn't look away and gives no sign of reconsidering. "Whatever they throw at me, I can take it."

"You say that now."

"I won't flake out on you." He thrusts his chin forward, and everything about his stance screams of determination. I've got no idea why he's so dead set on this, but in this moment, I truly believe he means what he says.

I take a few seconds to appraise him. I've never thought of Jimmy as anything other than a training buddy. I make a point not to check out the guys I train with because it's easier to stay focused if I think of them as totally nonsexual entities. But I suppose I've known him for a few months now and never stopped to really see him.

He's lean, on the tall side of average, and has hooded blue eyes that seem to see right through me. They're unnerving. His dirty-blond hair is tied at the nape of his neck, and it's even longer than mine. He looks like any other fighter in his early twenties, except for the lack of tattoos. As far as I can tell, he has virgin skin, which makes him an oddity in our line of work. An oddity like me. It's not that I've never thought of getting a tattoo, but my sponsors like the girl-next-door look, and if I started getting ink, it would mess with that image. Considering they're responsible for a large portion of my livelihood, I go along with it. I won't be a fighter forever, and if I want tattoos down the track, it's never too late. Hell, my grandma just had a butterfly tattooed on her arm.

I cock my head. Jimmy is cute. He's also fun and dedicated to MMA. It's not beyond the realm of possibility that we'd be together. If I bring him along as my date, my family probably won't think anything of it. But then, there is that one thing….

"I'm too old for you," I tell him. He looks young for his age, which makes the difference even more obvious.

He lifts an eyebrow. "Are you nuts?"

"I'd like to think not, but with my family, who knows?"

He shakes his head in disbelief. "You're fucking gorgeous. Six years means nothing. You'd still be the most beautiful woman I know if you were six*teen* years older than me."

Something awakens in my stomach. A flutter of awareness. A flash of heat.

I shouldn't be flattered. Jimmy is the kind of guy who talks a lot of shit. But he looks sincere. Does he actually think I'm beautiful? I mean, I know I'm pretty enough. If I wasn't, my sponsors wouldn't be so concerned about my image. But it's rare for a man to make a move on me. My theory is I intimidate non-fighters and just don't really click with fighters in a romantic sense.

"Well, thanks." I sound stilted and awkward, but I don't know how to take the compliment. I'm used to having my technique praised, but not my looks. And definitely not by a fit twenty-two-year-old with a heated gaze. "Are you really sure about this?"

"Yes." He steps forward. "Unless you'd rather go on five blind dates. If that's what you want, I'll leave right now. No problem."

"It's not." Especially not when I have a big fight coming up against the reigning British champion in my weight class. I need to focus all my attention on that. I've had many massive opportunities in the past few years, and I've always fallen short at the last hurdle. This is my chance to change that, and he's offering to help. The fluttering in my stomach morphs into a full-on tumble of nerves, but I find Kelsey's number in my phone and hit the Call button. "Hey, Kels. Sorry about cutting the call short."

"Oh my God!" she shrieks. "Who was that guy? He sounded hot. Is he hot?"

I exhale slowly and glance at Jimmy. "Yeah, he's hot."

His lips twist into a satisfied smirk that does ridiculous things to my insides.

"His name is Jimmy Parker. I've been seeing him for a little while now, and I didn't want to say anything because it's so new, but he's the reason I can't do any blind dates."

Kelsey squeals and I draw the phone away from my ear before she deafens me. My baby sister doesn't have any volume control. "Are you bringing him? You'd better be. Because I want to meet him, and Mom will too."

And so would Emma, Maryanne, Pru, and Del. Within an hour, I'd no doubt hear from each of my siblings. They're an interfering crew. Normally, I love them for it, but sometimes they take it too far.

"Yes, I'm bringing him. So if you could tell everyone to cancel whatever blind dates they've set up, that would be great. Jimmy is a fighter, so I doubt anyone wants to go head-to-head with him."

"So hot," Kelsey whispers, and I can practically hear her fanning herself. "Consider them canceled. Please tell me he has good-looking friends."

I laugh at the thought of my exuberant sister fluttering her eyelashes at the guys from Crown MMA. Unfortunately for her, they don't generally mess with the family of their training buddies. "If you come to Vegas, I'd be happy to introduce you, but if you're hoping for a sexy new boyfriend, you might be out of luck."

"Such a killjoy," she mutters. "I'd better go help Maryanne with her homework. See you soon. I can't wait to meet your man."

I catch Jimmy's eye and smile. "Yeah, he can't wait to meet you either." We say goodbye, then Jimmy and I head toward our cars together. "You're in for it now," I tell him. "Just wait. Nothing can prepare you for an inquisition by the Sears girls."

He lifts a shoulder nonchalantly. "Bring it on."

2

Jimmy

I study myself in the mirror. I can't believe I'm doing this. I've had my hair trimmed, I've shaved, and I'm dressed in a pair of tidy-casual pants and a button-down shirt that are fresh from the shop. I want to make a good first impression on Enya's family. But despite the new clothes and polished facade, all I can see is a trailer park kid staring back at me, trying a little too hard to look like he belongs. Unfortunately, this is the best it's going to get, so I turn away and finish packing my suitcase. I'm bringing my nicest suit —which cost more than a month of wages—but it's worth it because it makes me feel like I fit in when I'd otherwise be way out of my depths.

Today, we're flying to Wisconsin, and other than sorting out the travel details and dress code, Enya and I haven't talked about it much—a fact that definitely doesn't help my nerves. I pull the zipper closed and stand the suitcase up. After a quick check of the apartment, I head to the parking lot where my car is waiting. I volunteered to pick up Enya on the way to the airport because I know she thinks of me as a kid, and letting her see I have my own car that I keep in pristine condition might be the start of changing that. I plug the address into my phone and follow the directions to her place.

Enya lives in a two-story townhouse with no yard, but there's a collection of flowers growing in a planter box on the front porch. I park on the side of the road, head to the door, and knock. A few moments later, the door swings open and she appears in the doorway, towing a bag behind her, with another slung over her shoulder.

"Right on time," she says, flashing a grin that makes my heart stampede. A fluffy white cat winds between her legs, and she lets go of the suitcase to pat it on the head.

"You have a cat?" I've never heard her mention a pet. It feels like the sort of thing I ought to know.

"This is Daisy." She scoops the cat up with one arm and holds her out. Daisy gives me a bored look but doesn't seem annoyed so I tentatively pet her.

"Will she be okay alone for the weekend?" I ask.

Enya kisses Daisy's head, then sets her down and shuffles through the door, leaving the cat inside. "Tempe is going to drop by and feed her. She'll be fine."

"Good." Temperance Larson is one of the women we train with. She moved to Crown MMA Gym to learn from Harley, although she and Enya have become good friends too. I guess as women in a male-dominated sport, they formed some kind of bond. The three of them are always training or chatting. I like Tempe. She's nice, has a sense of humor, and she's never looked down on me.

Enya scans my attire. "I've never seen you turned out like this before."

Heat creeps up my cheeks and I clear my throat. "If I'm going to be your plus one, I should do a decent job of it." Hopefully such a good job that she decides to keep me around. "The car is over here." I lead her to it and pop the trunk so we can pack her luggage inside.

She climbs into the passenger seat and looks around. "Mine is nowhere near this clean."

"Thanks." A burst of pride warms my chest. Even if my ride isn't the newest or the flashiest, I keep it well maintained and appreciate her noticing. Growing up in a trailer park meant I didn't have nice things, so I never take any of my belongings for granted.

While we drive to the airport, we rehash yesterday's training session. Then, once we've checked in and are waiting to board, the conversation turns personal.

"We should get to know each other better," Enya says.

Panic spikes, sending a surge of adrenaline to my limbs. I can't tell her about my background yet. I've kept it close to my chest with everyone from the gym —other than Seth, our coach, who also grew up poor and understands my situation. I need time to get Enya to like me enough that my past no longer matters before I spill my secrets.

"My favorite color is blue." I feel stupid as soon as I've said it, but it's a diversion from the direction my thoughts were heading. "My best friend's name is Zane. My favorite food is sushi."

"Huh." She looks surprised. "I would have thought you were more of a steak guy."

I shrug. "I don't mind a good steak, but I prefer sushi." Mostly because the ability to buy it shows how far I've come. Sushi wasn't something anybody ever ate at the Twisted Willows Trailer Park. "What's your favorite color?" As if I haven't memorized everything she's ever said.

"Green." She opens her mouth to say something else, but at that moment we're invited to board. Thank fucking God. But my reprieve is only temporary. As soon as we're settled into our seats in business class—which she insisted on paying for—she picks up where we left off. "I should tell you more about my family so you're not blindsided. They can be a lot to handle."

"Okay."

"I have five siblings. My brother, Del, is the oldest. He's taken over the day-to-day management of Mom and Dad's dairy farm. Emma is next. She's the one getting married. She's an elementary school teacher. Her fiancé, Derek, is a teacher too. Then there's me. I'm a year younger than Emma, but because of our names and how similar we look, people often think we're twins."

"Emma and Enya," I muse. "Your parents didn't think too closely about that, did they?"

She rolls her eyes. "Apparently they thought it'd be cute. Anyway, it is what it is. My sister, Pru, is twenty-five. She's an accountant and she's in line to take over the local firm when the current accountant retires."

My eyebrows jump up. Her family sounds so different from mine. Farmers, teachers, accountants. It's all very white picket fence. So different from where I come from. "Sounds like a smart woman."

"She is," Enya agrees. "By far the most ambitious of us."

I give her a look. "You realize you're about to fight the reigning British women's champion, right? How is that not ambitious?"

"I just do what I love." Her tone is dismissive, and it makes me want to demand she recognize how extraordinary she is. "I don't care about being a big shot. I just want to get a fucking win. I think I deserve that after the past few years of so-close-but-not-quite."

"You do." Sensing she doesn't want to talk about it anymore, I continue, "So that must leave two more siblings?"

"Yes." She seems relieved I'm not persisting. "Kelsey is a baker. Maryanne is the baby. She's a senior in high school. She's currently going through a crisis because she doesn't know what she wants to do when she graduates."

"I get that." It was pure luck I found my career path. "But she's got plenty of time to figure it out."

Enya laughs. "Don't tell her that or she'll take your head off."

"I'm not scared of a teenage girl."

She chuckles in a way that makes me think perhaps I should be. "That's my family. Tell me about yours." Her brow furrows. "I don't think I've heard you mention them before."

My stomach lurches. I press clammy palms to my pants. "Nothing much to tell."

"Come on, Jimmy."

Ugh, I hate when she says my name. It makes me want to give her everything she asks for. But if I tell her the truth, she'll see me differently. I don't want to risk it. But if I want something real with her, I can't start out with a lie. We need a strong foundation, and she'll have to find out about my parents at some point.

Taking a deep breath, I gather more courage than I've ever needed in the cage. "My dad is permanently unemployed and angry. He likes to use his fists. Mom is a drunk. They still live in the trailer park where I grew up. Or at least, I think they do. I haven't spoken to them since I left after high school."

I force myself to keep my eyes open and take her reaction like a man. Whatever it is, I'll deal with it.

Enya

My heart breaks for Jimmy. The poor guy looks like he's expecting me to lash out after his revelation. As if knowing he was raised in that environment and still made it to his current position could possibly make me think less of him. "I'm so sorry you went through that."

His gaze skitters down to his lap. "I survived. I didn't tell you because I want you to feel sorry for me." His defensive tone indicates he's preparing for an argument.

"I know."

He deflates. "Really?"

"Yeah." I hesitate before adding anything else. Something tells me this man has a lot of pride, and if I mess up my response, he'll shut down. "You must be proud of everything you've accomplished." He probably had to work twice as hard as his peers.

He rubs his jaw. "I have a long way to go. I'm not out of the woods yet."

"I think you are," I declare because someone needs to have faith in him. "You're talented, and Seth wouldn't have invited you to Crown MMA if he didn't think you have the potential to be a champion."

He smiles, and it lights up his deep blue eyes. Awareness punches me in the gut, but I ignore it. The last thing I need is to get tingles over a man who's effectively my teammate.

"That means a lot." His husky voice tickles the edges of my nerves.

I try to shift away from him so I'm not tempted to investigate the strange new attraction I'm sensing between us, but there's only so far I can go without falling off my seat. "No problem." I search for a safe conversation topic, and my mind settles on something he said before. His father liked to use his fists. The full horror of the statement causes an ache in my bones as I realize that's probably how Jimmy learned to take a hit and keep on going. His ability to bounce back has always impressed me. No matter what the older guys throw, he never stops. No wonder.

He grabs his water bottle, and I notice his knuckles are white, so I decide not to press about his abusive father.

"I've got a great story to tell you about my brother." I launch into a monologue about the time Del tried to woo his high school sweetheart by organizing a dozen goats with bouquets tied to their necks to be dropped off at her family's barn on Valentine's Day. Her family owned a goat farm, and he'd gotten it into his head that including goats in his gift would make it more special. Only the goats had, of course, eaten the bouquets, and he'd been delayed at school, so there had been no one to explain the shipment of goats to her very confused parents. Then, once he'd gotten around to explaining himself, it turned out his girlfriend didn't find the idea of a dozen goats quite as romantic as he'd imagined.

"Did they break up?" Jimmy asks, completely absorbed in the story.

"Yes, and she told all of her friends, so everyone at school started calling him Goat Boy. I think some of the locals still do."

"Ouch." He winces with sympathy. "That's rough. Sounds like his heart was in the right place."

"It was." Although I can't help but giggle at the memory of twelve goats with chewed-off stalks around their necks. "But now he's found a woman who loves farming and livestock as much as him. I think if he gave Beth a posse of goats as a gift, she'd swoon with delight."

"Beth." He repeats the name as though committing it to memory. "Is she his wife?"

"Fiancée. Their wedding is in April." It's on the tip of my tongue to ask if he'd like to be my date to that wedding too, but something holds me back. I'm finding Jimmy a little more charming than expected, and I can't afford to have thoughts like that. My dating history has proved I don't have the time or energy to dedicate to a relationship. Too many men have tried to make me choose between them and my career, so it doesn't matter if he thinks I'm beautiful, or if his words make me feel giddy. It's a nonstarter.

"What are you thinking about?" he asks. "You're blushing."

I wrinkle my nose and inwardly curse. "Nothing important." But then I remember something else and curse out loud. "Fuck. We're going to have to share a bed."

"W-what?" He breaks into a coughing fit and clutches his throat. "You and me, in the same bed, together?"

"Yeah." I can't believe I didn't think of it earlier. "They're going to assume we're already sleeping together."

His entire face glows red, and he stammers something. My insides turn mushy because of how adorable he is. Damn him.

"Are your parents conservative?" he asks.

"Nope. They'll gladly give us a bed and hope it'll encourage you to stick around."

His eyes widen. "You think they'd want that?"

"Well, yeah. They've been trying to get me a man for years. They like the idea of having someone to look out for me since I live so far from them." They just don't seem to see why it never ends well. I just can't manage to hold onto a boyfriend while staying at the top of my game.

"Makes sense."

"In a twisted way." My eyes flutter closed, and for a few seconds, I allow myself to wonder what it would feel like to cuddle Jimmy's lean, muscular body in bed. He smells great, and I'd love to bury my face in the juncture of his neck and shoulder and breathe him in.

No, my subconscious reminds me. *You don't get a happily ever after. At least, not yet.*

There's a reason I don't date anymore. My last two boyfriends told me I didn't prioritize them enough. They hated that I was always training. They wanted the status of dating America's darling of MMA without the nuisance of all the work needed to maintain that position.

But, a voice at the back of my mind whispers, *Jimmy is a fighter too. He gets it. He won't make you feel bad for having dreams.*

I shouldn't even think about it, but suddenly, Jimmy Parker is infiltrating my thoughts, and I'm not sure I want that to change.

3

Jimmy

"Welcome to Cannondale, Wisconsin," Enya declares as we pass through a village that consists of a diner, a gas station, and a small collection of houses. She's driving since she's the one who knows where we're going. "Population: not enough."

"Is this where you grew up?" I ask, eager to learn as much as I can about her.

"Yep." She gestures at a long, narrow building as we near the other end of town, having taken all of thirty seconds to drive through it. "I went to Cannondale School. It goes from kindergarten right through to high school. There was something like a hundred students while I was there, and only five of them were my age."

I whistle. "Wow." It's hard to imagine her in a place like this. She's so suited to the city. "I bet prom was fun with only five of you."

She glances at me. "We didn't have prom. How about you? Did you have a cute date to the school dance?"

"Ha." I huff. "I couldn't afford nice clothes, so it was a nonstarter."

"Sorry."

I don't respond. I don't need her sympathy. But her reassurance wouldn't go astray because the closer we get to her family's farm, the more my nerves multiply. I want to make a good impression. I hope to spend many more years with her family.

"Remind me of who's going to be there."

"All of my siblings, my parents, Grandma Jo, and possibly some aunts and uncles. I'm not a hundred percent sure."

"Wow." Her family sounds so different from my apathetic parents that I've got no idea how to fit in with them, but I'll do my best because I'll be damned if that's the reason Enya doesn't see me as someone she could date for real.

"I warned you they could be a lot to handle," she mutters, "but you were determined to come."

"No regrets."

She pulls onto a side road a few miles out of town, and we travel down it for several minutes. I'm too nervous to chat, so I mentally gather myself. She seems to be doing the same. Eventually, a large white house appears on the horizon. As we draw nearer, I can see the dark green trim of the windowsills and door-frames. It looks like a homestead from a movie. Welcoming and idyllic.

"It's really nice," I murmur.

Enya peers through the windshield as though trying to see what I can. "I suppose so. I'm used to it, so I probably take it for granted."

I shake my head. I could never take a place like this for granted. It's everything I didn't have growing up and only makes the differences between us more pronounced.

"You okay?" she asks.

"Yeah."

We turn onto a gravel drive and crunch along the well-maintained surface until the house looms over us.

Enya parks and we climb out of the car. "Brace yourself."

I'm about to ask what she means when the front door opens and four young women race toward us. My eyes go wide. Holy shit. The one in front squeals and throws herself at us.

"Hiiiii!" she yells, squeezing her sister in a bone-crushing hug. "You're back! Oh my gosh. It's so good to see you."

Based on the level of noise and what I know about Enya's family, I suspect this is Kelsey.

Enya hugs her back. "Good to see you too, Kels."

Yes. Nailed it.

I scan the other sisters, who are waiting behind Kelsey. I identify Emma straightaway, based on Enya's comment about their similarities. Emma is slightly shorter and more willowy, but otherwise their features match in a lot of ways. Beside Emma is a girl with dark blonde hair held off her face by a pink headband. I'd guess she's still in her teens, so I assume this is Maryanne. That means the other one, clad in a form-fitting black dress, must be Pru. I smile at each of them in turn, feeling nauseous as I wonder what they see when they look at me. Someone who's a decent guy for their sister? Or a trailer trash kid who isn't fit to clean her shoes?

Kelsey opens her eyes and spots me over Enya's shoulder. She releases her sister and rushes over. I have two seconds to steel myself before she sweeps me into the same tight embrace she subjected Enya to. "You must be Jimmy. I'm so glad you're here." Her voice is too loud beside my ear, but I manage not to flinch. She pulls back, still holding my upper arms, and looks me up and down. "Yes, you'll do." She drops her hands and turns to Enya. "You were right. He's hot."

My cheeks flame. What the…?

"Kels!" Enya swats her sister's shoulder. "You're embarrassing him."

"Oh, sorry." She glances back at me. "I tend not to think before I speak. I know it's a bad habit, but I don't bother changing because my family have to love me the way I am. It's, like, a requirement."

"Nice to meet you. Kelsey, right?"

"Right." She waves a hand behind her. "And that's Emma, Maryanne, and Pru." She turns to Enya. "Mom, Dad, and Del waited inside. They didn't want to overwhelm your boyfriend."

Boyfriend.

I meet Enya's eyes and something flares to life between us. An electric connection that defies words. I want so badly to fulfill that role. I only hope she can't see my yearning written across my face. But then I glimpse something similar in hers. A hint of longing, gone before I can be sure it's there.

Emma steps forward, appraising me. "Enya has never introduced us to a boyfriend since she left Cannondale." She offers a hand. When I take it, she grips a little more firmly than necessary. "I hope you're treating my sister well."

I hold her gaze, unflinching. "If I ever don't, you've got permission to take a free shot at my face."

Her lips lift at the corners. "I'll hold you to that."

I approach the next sister. "Maryanne?"

"Yes." She grins, apparently delighted. "I hope Enya only told you the good stuff about me."

"Of course." I wink. "It's all good stuff, right?"

"Pfft. Totally."

The last sister, Pru, thrusts a hand forward and doesn't look nearly so charmed by my attempts to be friendly. "If you mess with her, I'll find every single skeleton in your closet."

A shiver runs down my spine, but I shake her hand anyway and pretend not to be disturbed. "I won't mess with her." I lower my voice so Enya can't hear. "She means everything to me."

"Good. Keep it that way." Then she flashes a smile. "Come in. Mom and Dad can't wait to meet you."

***

Enya

So far, so good. I grab Jimmy's hand and pause, surprised by how much larger it is than mine. He's hardly the biggest guy at the gym, so I suppose I take his size for granted, but he's still taller and broader than me. His skin is rough from the callouses he earned doing pullups and using a weight bar. When our palms brush together, awareness flows up my arm, and it's all I can do not to drop his hand and back the hell away. I've never had this kind of reaction to a man. Why is it happening now?

Maryanne skips along ahead of us, and I focus on the way her hair bounces on her back to take my mind off the fact I'm weirdly attracted to Jimmy. My training buddy. My *friend*. We enter the foyer and I slip off my shoes. Jimmy follows suit. Maryanne leads us through the kitchen, to our left, and into the living area, where my parents, Grandma Jo, Del, and Beth are seated on the sofas and armchairs.

"Welcome home, darling." Mom stands and glides over. She's every bit the hostess, which is funny when I recall all the times I've seen her covered in farm muck and stinking to high heaven. The ease with which she switches roles has always impressed me. I let her pull me into a hug and breathe in her scent. She smells like flowers and my childhood. "I hope your trip went smoothly."

"Yes, thanks." I kiss her cheek and draw back. "Mom, this is my… Jimmy." I can't bring myself to call him my boyfriend when it's not true. Saying he's my date is acceptable, but I'm not comfortable adding to the lie.

Jimmy offers her a hand. His shoulders are back, and I've never seen him look quite so much like he's standing in front of a firing squad. "Thank you for having me, Mrs. Sears. It's a pleasure to meet you."

Mom beams at him. "The pleasure is all mine, Jimmy." She pumps his hand enthusiastically. "Call me Martha. Does Jimmy stand for something? James, perhaps?"

"No, ma'am." He gives her a pained look. "I wish it did, but Jimmy is the name on my birth certificate."

Mom nods, clearly unsure how to take that. "How unique. But I'd best not hog your attention." She waves a hand toward Dad. "This is my husband, Edwin. Beside him is our eldest, Del, and his fiancée, Beth." Jimmy nods to each of them deferentially. He's going to have them eating out of his hand in no time. "Over here is Grandma Jo." She leans closer and stage whispers, "Pay no attention to anything she says. Nobody else does."

"Oh phooey!" Grandma Jo exclaims. "I'm the only one in this nuthouse brave enough to say what they think." She grabs her glasses from the coffee table and sits them atop the bridge of her nose. "Come closer, boy." Jimmy edges toward her, sending me a worried look. Grandma Jo peruses him thoroughly from head to toe. "Very nice," she says, and sits back in her chair. "You've scored yourself a Kurt Cobain lookalike, Enya. Nice ass too. I always knew you'd be the one to do me proud."

My jaw drops. After a lifetime of Grandma Jo's inappropriate comments, I should be immune, but being away from her has made my memory foggy. I'm about to scold her (albeit good-naturedly) when Jimmy winks at her.

"Now I see why Enya is such a boss babe. How could she not be, with you for a grandmother?"

Grandma Jo squints at him, trying to decide whether he's teasing, but then she nods. "Damn straight. I'm the O.G. Isn't that what the kids say these days?"

I snort and hope she doesn't notice. "Don't encourage her. That's the last thing she needs."

Grandma Jo scoffs. "If the handsome young man wants to shower me with flattery, please let him." She bats her eyelashes. "I don't get opportunities like this all the time."

I sigh. It seems Jimmy is a hit. Hopefully we can keep it that way. I'd hate to see how my family would react if they learned the truth about our relationship.

"So." Del holds up a game box. "Now that you're here, we can start Monopoly. Teams of two. I'm with Beth, obviously."

Dragging a palm down my face, I swallow a pang of guilt for not warning Jimmy about game night. I love my family to bits, but any one of them would sell their own grandmother if it meant getting a property they want in Monopoly. They're fiercely competitive.

I step closer to Jimmy. "You know how to play, right?"

"I'm better at cards," he murmurs. "But I know the rules."

"I'm with Jimmy," I announce before anyone else has the opportunity to harass him.

"Aw." Maryanne pouts. "But I wanted a new partner. I'm sick of being with Pru. She uses her calculator for everything."

Pru holds up a finger to silence her. "But we win."

"Usually," Mom adds. "Not always. Don't get over-confident, Prudence."

I roll my eyes. And thus, the drama begins.

Kelsey partners with Emma, Dad with Grandma Jo, and Mom decides to sit it out so she can prepare dinner. Del sets up the board on the coffee table, and we arrange ourselves in a circle around it—some of us on the floor, while Grandma Jo stays in her chair, which Dad drags over to the table.

"Where's Derek tonight?" I ask, noticing he's absent.

"The groom can't see the bride before the wedding," Kelsey recites in a singsong manner.

"He and his friends are at our place," Emma says. "They're drinking beer and watching football. Both of us wanted a low-key night. Tomorrow will be busy enough."

The game begins, and with each roll of the dice, my family reveals a little more of their crazy. At first, Jimmy is reserved, but as the game progresses, he starts teasing the others and gaining confidence in our moves. I can't help sneaking peeks at him when he's not looking. He really is a cute guy. Especially when he smiles. I never realized how rarely he does. Usually he'll smirk or half smile, but his full smile hits me like a sucker punch every time.

Emma leaps to her feet. "I've got to go to the ladies' room." She grabs my elbow. "Enya, join me."

I cock a brow as she drags me into the library. Clearly, she just wants to gossip in private. "What do you need to talk to me about?"

"Jimmy." She sighs happily. "He's perfect. He completely adores you."

I frown. "He does?"

"Absolutely." She shakes her head as though she can't believe I'm so blind. "Whenever you're not looking at him, he's looking at you. He's got it bad."

My interest stirs. Emma is observant. She has to be in order to teach children. If she thinks Jimmy has been stealing glances at me, then he probably has. Which begs the question: does he want more than this fake arrangement between us? I'd thought it was strange how he volunteered to be my date, but if he's hoping to spend more time with me, it makes perfect sense. Jimmy is a confident guy, though. If he wanted to ask me out, wouldn't he just go ahead and do it? But then my mind flicks back to how vulnerable he seemed when he was telling me about his parents. Perhaps he's not as cocky as he appears. Maybe it's an act. Whatever the case, I'll be paying much closer attention when we return to the living room.

"You approve of him?" I ask because I value Emma's opinion. She's the only one of my sisters who's successfully found a great guy so far.

"I'd consider myself cautiously optimistic," she replies. "I've only just met him, but I'm getting good vibes, and I know the others are too."

"Thanks, Em." I reach out and squeeze her shoulder. "That means a lot."

Now I just need to figure out whether I want to see if there could be something real between us. I'm not even sure if a relationship is a possibility, considering the epic fight on my horizon. It's a chance for redemption. I can't screw that up. Not for any guy, no matter how tempting. My boyfriends have always had a habit of dropping ultimatums, and even though I don't think Jimmy is that sort of person, I don't want to risk it. I've been wrong before, and those breakups have left invisible scars.

Over the course of the night, I confirm Emma is right. Jimmy does look at me every chance he gets. Except for when it's time to get ready for bed. Suddenly, we're alone in my childhood room, having said goodnight to everyone else, and it seems like he's incapable of looking anywhere except the floor. He shuffles into the attached bathroom, and I hear the shower start. I change into my pajamas and climb into bed. It's king-size but feels small for two people. I get out again and find a couple of extra pillows, which I stuff down the center beneath the blankets.

When Jimmy emerges in a billow of steam, my mouth goes dry. Low-slung sweatpants hug his legs, and his leanly muscled torso ripples as he pads toward me. He has a lot of abs. I've seen them before but never let myself really *look*. Now, I can't seem to help it. I'm helpless as my gaze traces the rounded muscles of his shoulders and pecs, down to the ridges of his abdomen. My lady parts hum to life. Dear God, I have to share a bed with *that*?

One side of his mouth tugs up in a smirk. "Like what you see?"

I snap my mouth closed. "You're toned... and stuff."

I can't for the life of me string a sensible sentence together.

He glances at the bed and his brows draw together as he notices the pillow barrier. "Are you worried I might get handsy?"

No. I'm worried I might.

It's been a long time since anything other than a vibrator was between my legs. I nearly moan as Jimmy slips beneath the blankets opposite me and his clean, masculine scent fills my nostrils.

Behave, Enya.

I reach up and switch off the light. As I lie on my back, I can hear him breathing. His inhales and exhales are slow and steady. Clearly this situation isn't getting to him as much as it is to me.

"Your family are great," he says, breaking the silence. "You're lucky to have them."

I roll onto my side, my back to him, and curl my knees up to my chest, berating myself for fantasizing about him when he's probably having perfectly innocent thoughts. "I am. They're a little overwhelming at times, but I wouldn't have them any other way."

He doesn't respond and I wonder if he's thinking about his own family, which sounds as far from mine as it gets. Suddenly, I wish I could offer to lend him mine. He deserves to experience love like theirs. Somehow, I know that's something he's never had. But I can't fix that for him.

"Sweet dreams."

His voice is the last thing I hear before I drift off to sleep. "Goodnight, beautiful."

4

JIMMY

I wake slowly, enjoying the warmth of the bed and the softness of the woman in my arms.

Hang on. The woman in my arms?

I blink and glance down at Enya, who's nestled against my chest. My hard cock is aligned with her ass. Shit. I was having a really good dream, and I must have made a move on her during the night. I extricate myself carefully. As I reach the edge of the bed, I realize I wasn't the one to breach the pillow barrier. *She* was. My dick pulses at the thought that she sought me out. Conscious or not, she wanted to be near me, and that counts for something, right?

My hormones seem to think so. My erection strains against my lower abdomen, desperate for relief. I shouldn't be surprised. After years of having a celebrity crush on her, followed by months of actually knowing her, my body is fully committed to wanting what it can't have. I sigh and turn away from the bed, willing my hard-on to deflate. When it doesn't, I resign myself to the fact I'm going to have to jerk off in the shower. I head into the bathroom, close the door, and start the water. Once it's heated, I strip off my sweatpants and get in, immediately fisting my cock. I close my eyes and imagine what Enya's supple body might look like beneath her clothes. I've seen her in booty shorts and a crop top before, so I don't have to work too hard to picture the rest. But what color would her nipples be? Based on her pale skin and freckles, I think a dusky shade of rose.

Fuck.

I slick my hand with soap and pump ruthlessly. I shouldn't enjoy this. I just need to get it out of my system, so I can act like a normal human rather than a horny kid. It doesn't take much to have me on the verge of coming. Mouth hanging open, I pant as pleasure coils at the base of my spine. Just as I'm about to crash over the edge, the door clicks open. I stare at the entrance as Enya appears. She stops short, her eyes wide. I squeeze the base of my cock and turn my body away from her, but my orgasm is already upon me. I groan as the evidence of what I've been doing splatters on the shower floor.

Damn.

I rest my head against the wall, humiliation threatening to consume me. Any hope of convincing Enya I'm more mature than she thinks has gone out the window. Hopefully I haven't completely ruined my chances of winning her over, although it wouldn't surprise me if she has trouble looking me in the eye after this. When I finally risk a glance at the door, it's shut. I clean myself, wash down the shower, and turn the water off. I take my time toweling dry and cross my fingers she's already left to use another shower because surely, she can't want to use this one. I wrap the towel around my hips and open the door, wincing when I spot her sitting on the edge of the bed.

She leaps to her feet. "I'm *so* sorry. I was on autopilot. I didn't hear the shower. I swear I didn't mean to creep on you."

Hang on, she thinks *she's* the creep in this situation?

"I'm so, so sorry," she repeats, her cheeks coloring as she steals a peek at my crotch. "So sorry."

Okay, well that's not good for my ego. "Don't worry about it." I duck my head. "Please forget everything. Wipe your mind clean."

"Uh…."

I glance up in time to see her smile impishly.

"I'm not sure I want to go that far," she says. "Just so you know, you have nothing to be ashamed of."

I narrow my eyes. Is she commenting on my dick? I'm really not sure how to take that. "Thanks, I guess." This has gone past awkward. I grab my suitcase from the floor and drag it back to the bathroom. "I'll just get changed."

Fortunately, when I emerge a few minutes later, Enya is gone. I wander downstairs and find Emma, Del, Beth, Martha, and Edwin in the dining room.

"Happy wedding day," I tell Emma.

"Thank you." She smiles. "I'm looking forward to it. Derek and I have been together for a long time, so getting married doesn't actually seem like that big of a deal. It's just making everything official."

Del laughs. "Then why do you need a princess dress and professional hair and makeup?"

She shoots him a glare. "Because that's what I want."

He exchanges a look with Beth. "We're going to have a small ceremony out by the barn in summer. Just family and a couple of close friends."

Emma's expression softens and she addresses Beth, ignoring her brother. "That sounds perfect for you."

"I hope so," Beth replies.

"Good morning, Jimmy," Martha cuts in. She gestures at the selection of food in the center of the table. "Help yourself. Did you sleep well?"

My face heats as I recall waking up wrapped around her daughter. "Yes, thank you."

Emma giggles, clearly noticing my discomfort, but no one else says anything. I stack eggs, bacon, and toast onto a plate and sit beside Emma.

"So, Jimmy." Edwin catches my eye over the rim of his coffee mug. "Enya tells us you're a fighter at her gym."

I swallow a mouthful of egg before responding. "Yeah. I've been there for over a year now. It's a great gym, and Seth is the best coach in Vegas."

Emma shudders. "I've never understood why Enya would want to fight for a living."

My lips twist because I definitely understand. "She's an adrenaline junkie. Getting in the cage with someone gives you a pretty major high."

A coffee mug appears in front of me, and I glance up. Martha smiles. "I thought you might like one."

"Thank you." I'm oddly touched. In that moment, I get a taste of what it might be like to be part of this family. I like it. In fact, I crave it. I only hope I'm not taunting myself with the thing I want most because if the Sears ever find out I've deceived them, they might not want anything to do with me, and I couldn't blame them for that.

Enya

I shut myself in the room Del and Beth are using and sink to the floor with my back against the door. The persistent throbbing between my legs won't stop. I can't get the image of Jimmy's hard cock out of my head. I wish I'd been able to see his face as he lost control. I know that makes me a perve, but as much as I regret making things awkward between us, seeing him like that was the hottest experience of my life.

I take my phone from the pocket of my robe and find Tempe's number. She's become one of my closest girlfriends during the months we've been training together since we each moved to Crown MMA from our former gyms. I hesitate for a moment, wondering if spilling my feelings to her is a good idea, but then I hit Call. She won't say anything to anyone. She's one of the most loyal people I know.

"Morning." Tempe's voice is sharp and clear. Even though it's a couple of hours earlier back home, she's always up first thing. "Daisy says hi too. Is everything good at the family farm?"

"I saw Jimmy naked."

"Uh." I can picture the crease between her dark brows as she tries to figure out how to respond to that. "Was it good?"

I snort-laugh. "That's what you want to know?"

"Well, yeah." I can hear the grin in her voice. "Second-hand details about naked men are the closest thing I've come to getting action in ages."

I file that away under interesting information. Apparently all is not good between Tempe and her boyfriend.

"He's seriously hot," I confess. "But that's not the worst part."

"Then what is?" She sounds intrigued.

"He was, you know." I squirm, not sure how to say it. "Touching himself."

At that, Tempe bursts out laughing. "Are you saying he was jacking off?"

"In the shower," I confirm.

"And you interrupted?"

"I walked in right in time to witness the grand finale."

She giggles, and I feel like a teenage girl again. "I'm not surprised he had to do that after spending a night with you. That man has had the world's most massive crush on you since day one."

"You think?" The image of him, naked and dripping, fills my mind again, and every female part of my body responds to it. Damn. When we devised this plan, I never expected to actually want to bang him.

"Please, girl." Her tone is rich with amusement. "If you think about it, it'll be obvious. The question is: are you interested in him too?"

I picture his hand shuttling over his erection and whimper. "*So* interested. But you know I can't afford to take my eyes off the prize."

"The prize being winning the transatlantic fight?"

"Exactly."

She's quiet for a moment, and I know she's thinking it over carefully. As a woman in MMA, she knows it can be difficult to get traction, so she won't dismiss my concerns the way my sisters might. "He's a fighter," she says finally. "Surely if you explain, he'll understand and be patient."

"Maybe." But I'm afraid to be hopeful.

"Honestly, En. I think he'd do nearly anything for a chance with you."

"Hmm." I want to see what could happen between us, but I also don't want to string him along or hurt him. He's too good of a guy for that. "Thanks. You've given me a lot to think about."

"No problem." There's a rustle in the background. "I've gotta get to training. Enjoy the wedding."

"I will. Bye, Tempe."

"See you later." She hangs up.

I return to my bedroom and find Jimmy has left. I rush through a cold shower, trying desperately to tamp down my libido and ignore the memories of him in here not that long ago, and then I get dressed. I head downstairs, following the sound of conversation to the dining room. Jimmy is seated around the table with several members of my family. He glances up and his smile lights the room. Having him here feels right. I smile back and take the seat beside him. A sense of déjà vu strikes me. As though we've done this before. Or perhaps it's a premonition of things to come.

I shut that thought down fast. It won't pay to get ahead of myself. Anything could go wrong before the end of the day, and knowing my family, it likely will.

5

Emma's wedding ceremony is at the local gardens. It's a cold day, so everyone is wearing coats over their dresses and shirts. Jimmy, Kelsey, and I are standing together near the rows of matching, white-draped chairs when I see a familiar face approaching.

I groan. "Emma invited Brad?"

Kelsey makes a face. "His parents have been friends with Mom and Dad for decades. It'd be weird if she didn't."

Much as I know she's right, I don't want to see my ex-boyfriend. He and I dated through high school, beginning when he was a sophomore and I was a freshman, and somehow, despite me training my ass off and talking constantly about becoming a professional athlete, he was still surprised when I told him I was moving to Las Vegas to pursue a career in MMA. Apparently, he'd thought I was all talk and I'd settle down and get a normal job after I graduated.

As if.

He was the first boyfriend who forced me to

choose between being with him and chasing my dream. The first, but by no means the last.

"Who's Brad?" Jimmy asks, but his scowl tells me he's guessed the answer.

"My ex."

"He's also one of the guys who was lined up to go on a blind date with you," Kelsey adds apologetically.

The bottom falls out of my stomach. "What? Who would think that's a good idea?"

"Pru." Kelsey rolls her eyes. "She had this idea of a grand reunion. I don't think she mentioned it to him, though. She thought it would be more romantic if it was a surprise."

I wince. I was never fully up front with my family about what happened between me and Brad. I know Pru means well, but sometimes I wonder how my sister can be so smart about some things and so clueless about others. I grab Jimmy's hand so he can't escape and leave me on my own. It might be unfair to ask it of him, but I need support right now.

"Sorry in advance for anything that douchebag might say."

He stiffens almost imperceptibly. "I can handle him."

In a fight, I have no doubt of that, but Brad's words are his weapon, and Jimmy is more vulnerable than he likes to let on.

"Hey, look. It's America's darling of MMA," Brad says as he draws near. His hair is trimmed neatly and he's wearing a suit that doesn't quite cover his slight paunch. Despite that, he looks good, for the most part. "It's great to see you, Enya. It's been a while."

Not long enough.

Even when we were dating, Brad had been callous, but considering the slim pickings in Cannondale, he'd seemed the best of the bunch. Now I wish I'd waited until I met someone I had more in common with before getting into a relationship.

"It has," I agree, silently cursing the fact it hasn't been longer. "Are you still living locally?"

He nods. "I'm working as a real estate agent over in Tuchette." He glances at Kelsey. "Hi, Kels." He ignores Jimmy and addresses me again. "I've been looking forward to the chance to connect with you. It's a shame you brought a date."

From the corner of my eye, I see Jimmy open his mouth, and I know whatever he's about to say won't be wedding-appropriate, so I squeeze his hand in warning and beat him to the punch.

"Jimmy is my boyfriend." Perhaps I hadn't wanted to claim him as such to my family, but things are changing between us, and I'm not about to let Brad belittle him.

Brad's face falls. He scans Jimmy from head to toe, and his expression twists into a nasty sneer. "You can't be serious about this white trash kid. Is he even legally allowed to drink?"

My mouth drops open, and a red haze descends over me. He did *not* just call Jimmy white trash to his face. I release Jimmy's hand and march toward Brad. Nobody gets away with saying something like that to a guy who's always been supportive of me. I hear Kelsey gasp as I jab my pointer finger into Brad's chest, but I can't understand what she's saying because there's a ringing in my ears blocking out everything except the person who insulted someone I care about.

"Take it back," I demand. "Jimmy is not white trash. He's a hard-working, fun, caring guy who overcame some pretty shitty circumstances to make something of himself." I barely resist the urge to gnash my teeth at him. "He's never made me feel like I'm not enough or that I'm wrong for having my own dreams. He's worth two of you. So don't you dare try to make him feel small because I promise, I'll make you regret it."

***

Jimmy

Does she really think that much of me?

I can't believe the way Enya flies to my defense. Nobody has ever done that before. I've always had to fight my own battles. But she's going toe to toe with a man twice her size for my sake.

Emotion swells in my chest, and I don't bother waiting to hear how Assface will respond. I grab her hand, yank her to me, and finally—*finally*—taste the lips I've been craving for months. They're soft against mine, unreactive at first, but as I sweep my tongue over them, they part on a sweet gasp. I moan against her mouth. She's fresh and minty from brushing her teeth before we left, but there's an underlying spice that's pure Enya. I gather her in my arms and revel in the perfect fit of our bodies. My heart sings as she responds, gripping my shirt tightly and pulling me closer.

Someone clears their throat. Embarrassed, but not enough to regret my actions, I detach from her and blink at my surroundings as they come into focus. But then, before I have a chance to figure out who made the sound, Enya grabs my chin and draws me into another kiss. My eyes flutter closed. I couldn't keep them open if I wanted to. I'm living in a dream. *Enya Sears* is kissing me. And this time, she started it. When she releases me, we're both breathing heavily. I gaze into her soft brown eyes, noticing her pupils are blown. She searches my face, and she looks surprised. I'm not. I always knew it would be like this between us.

"That was…." She trails off.

"Incredible," I suggest. "So fucking incredible. Thank you for standing up for me."

She cocks her head as though she's forgotten what happened before the kiss, and I can't help the smug smirk of satisfaction that steals over my face. "You deserve to be treated like you matter."

Kelsey clears her throat again. "Break it up, love-birds. The ceremony is about to start."

I glance up and see Brad has left. It's just Kelsey, Enya and I standing. Everyone else has taken a seat. My cheeks burn as we hurry over to a row of chairs near the front that are reserved for family. I sit on the end nearest the aisle, while Enya sits beside me, closer to the rest of her family. The groom waits at the altar with the officiant and the best man. Emma mentioned yesterday she'd decided not to have any family in the bridal party because her sisters would have turned it into a competition.

Enya's hand slips into mine, and I smile down at her. She leans closer and speaks near my ear. "That wasn't fake."

"No," I agree, beyond grateful she realizes it. "It was completely real."

She rubs a thumb over the back of my hand. "Let's talk later?"

"Yes." I like the sound of that. I press a kiss to the heel of her palm. She shivers, and my dick jams against the front of my trousers. Damn this suit. Although it's probably lucky I'm so restrained because if I were wearing my usual shorts, my hard-on would be far more obvious.

Music plays, and we stand as the flower girl appears, sprinkling petals on the grass. Once she reaches the front, she slides into a chair. The maid of honor follows, wearing a purple dress that brushes the ground as she walks. She stands near the officiant, opposite the best man. Emma comes last, gliding on Edwin's arm. She's resplendent in a white gown with a bunch of floaty layers that seem to shift as she walks. My heart expands at the thought that this is what Enya might look like on her wedding day. I doubt she'd opt for an outfit so princessy, but the sisters are alike enough that I can easily swap them out in my mind. My chest aches with how badly I want the vision to come true, but only if I'm the lucky bastard she's walking toward.

Tears fill my eyes as Edwin hands Emma to the man I assume is Derek. I swipe at them discreetly. Everything about this day is perfect. I'd never dreamed I could end up somewhere like this. Not back when I was dodging my father's fists and trying to make myself invisible on the ratty sofa bed in the back of our trailer. The whole scene could have been a fairytale for how far away it seems. But I'm here. I'm part of it. And I'm not white trash, whatever Enya's ex or the scared voice in my head might say.

The couple exchange vows, and I dab at the corners of my eyes when the damn things won't stop leaking.

"You okay?" Enya murmurs.

"Fine," I grumble. "It's just really nice, you know?"

"Aww, Jimmy." Her voice takes on a teasing tone. "Are you crying happy tears?"

"Maybe. But if you ever mention this, I'll never speak to you again." I'm bullshitting and we both know it.

She rests her head on my shoulder. "You've got

nothing to be ashamed of. You're sweet, and I love that about you."

Her words send a jolt of electricity through my veins. *Love.* That emotion has been out of reach for so long, and it's strange to hear the word. But finally, I'm beginning to feel hopeful. If Enya loves something about me, it's not so far-fetched to believe she might love *me*, full stop, one day.

We watch the rest of the ceremony in silence. Afterward, when we've said our congratulations to the newly married couple, we stroll through the gardens and I decide to take the initiative.

"I like you, Enya." I clasp her hand and swing it between us. "I want to take you out somewhere for a real date when we get back home. Would you be open to that?"

She grins from ear to ear. "If you kiss me the way you just did, I'll go anywhere you ask."

I stop moving and turn to face her. "Really? I know this isn't what we agreed."

She shrugs. "So what? I like you, and you like me. Isn't that enough of a reason to see where things go?"

"I hope so."

"But here's the thing."

Uh-oh. I should have known there'd be a but.

"I need to focus all of my energy on my next fight." She tucks her hair behind her ear with her free hand and shields her eyes from the glare while she looks at me. "I'm going to be training a lot, and I can't afford to have my attention divided."

"Okay." As long as she agrees to give me a genuine chance, I don't care what form it comes in.

"Okay?" she asks in disbelief. "That's it?"

I frown. "What did you want me to say?"

"I don't know," she mutters. "But I thought you'd

argue. I basically told you I won't have time for you for another few weeks."

"No big deal." I've waited this long for her. A little longer won't matter. "I can cook you dinner some days. You have to eat, right?"

She cocks her head. "That's not fair. I don't expect you to run around after me."

I roll my eyes. "It's not for long. I want to spend time with you, and I don't care what that looks like. I'm sure it won't be the last time one of us has to prioritize a fight. Someday, I'll have the kind of matches you do now, and I hope you won't hold it against me if I need to put in a few extra hours of training."

"Of course not."

I smile, amused by the crinkle of confusion between her brows. "Then we don't have a problem, do we?"

"I guess not." She steps closer and rests her cheek on my chest. "Now that's all sorted, can we kiss again?"

As if I'd ever say no to that. "Hell yeah."

6

A solid chest is pressed to my back. Long limbs encase my own, and a hand is positioned possessively over one of my breasts. I smile and keep my eyes closed, enjoying the sensation of Jimmy spooning me. We didn't bother with the pillow barrier last night, after the wedding, but we didn't do anything more than make out either. I'd been hornier than I'd ever been in my life, but Jimmy had rebuffed my advances, explaining clearly—and reasonably, damn him—that he wants to wait until we can explore a sexual relationship with a clean slate and none of this deception hanging over us. It was thoughtful, and that only made me want him more. I'd pouted and tried to grab his cock, thinking if I got him off, perhaps he'd return the favor, but he'd gently removed my hands and slept with what had to be an uncomfortable erection.

I wiggle away from him and roll over so I can study his drowsy face. He looks even younger when he sleeps. Insecurity pierces my confidence, but I remind myself six years isn't a lot in the grand scheme of things. Especially not when someone has as much life experience as he does. His jaw is relaxed, his hair mussed around his face. Stubble covers his cheeks and chin. It's mostly blond, but there are a couple of ginger hairs mixed in, which makes me smile. Del always gets sensitive when people point out the shades of red in his beard. I wonder if Jimmy is the same.

I gaze at his lips. They're full and soft. I trace an invisible line down his body. The smattering of gold hair on his chest makes my pussy clench. I want to run my fingers through it, but if I do, he might wake up, so I settle for mentally following the slope of his shoulder and upper arm to where they disappear beneath the blankets. With his toned but unblemished body and blond mane of hair, he seems to hearken back to early Anglo-Saxon ancestors.

"Hey." The rough greeting catches me by surprise, and my eyes dart to his face. He shifts closer to kiss me. "How'd you sleep?" His words carry a tenderness I don't expect, and I can't help but think there seems to be a sense of calm about him that's usually absent.

"Not bad, but it would've been better if I'd had an orgasm."

He chuckles, and then nuzzles the side of my face. When he pulls back, his smile absolutely destroys me. "I want to make sure we're ready. I couldn't handle it if we had a one-time thing."

"We won't," I assure him. Whether or not this attraction turns into anything long-term, neither of us can know for sure, but with how eager I am to learn more about him and to explore our physical connection, I know it won't be a one-night stand or a fling. And based on the way he looks at me, his feelings are already involved. The warmth that steals into the corners of my heart tells me mine are too. "But I understand where you're coming from." I roll away from him. "My parents are probably up. We should get breakfast and say goodbye." Our flight leaves in a few hours, and I don't feel like I've seen nearly enough of my family. I wish I could stay for longer. I'll have to come back during the downtime after my big fight.

I tug on some clothes and watch Jimmy dress, admiring the way his muscles ripple as he pulls a T-shirt over his head and slips on a pair of jeans. I'm not sure if he's growing more comfortable with my family, or if it's just that the formal part of the weekend is over, but either way, I'm glad he's starting to relax enough to be casual around them.

When we head out in search of people, most of the clan are gathered in the dining room—except for Emma and Derek, who left for parts unknown last night. Planning the honeymoon was Derek's contribution, and he stubbornly refused to divulge where they were going.

"Sleep late, did you?" Kelsey asks as I grab a plate and reach for a whole wheat bagel and a few slices of avocado. Training for a fight means eating carefully, both to ensure peak fitness and to make sure I'm beneath the weight limit for my category.

"Sleeping isn't what they were doing," Grandma Jo snickers. She holds out a fist for me to bump.

I shake my head, my cheeks flushing. "Sorry to disappoint, but we've been behaving perfectly respectably."

Jimmy raises an eyebrow, as if to remind me we weren't total angels, but I ignore him. Making out doesn't count. Not in Grandma Jo's book.

She sighs and makes a show of ogling him. "If you're not tapping that, it's a damn travesty."

"Okay, Grandma." Del plucks Grandma Jo's post-wedding mimosa from the table and passes it to Beth. "I think you've had enough."

Maryanne giggles. "You know it has nothing to do with the alcohol."

Grandma Jo winks at Maryanne. "Aimless cheerleader or not, you're the smart one."

Mom strides in with a pot of coffee and starts filling mugs. I grab one for myself and one for Jimmy, who's served himself waffles for breakfast. I give him the stink eye and bite reluctantly into my bagel. It tastes nothing like delicious waffles.

"Thank you, Martha." Jimmy glances around the table. "Are Edwin and Pru still sleeping?"

"Pru had to get some work done," Mom replies. "As for Edwin… let's just say he doesn't bounce back from a big night as well as he used to."

Maryanne's mouth drops open. "Dad is *hungover?*"

"Regrettably." Amusement lifts the corners of Martha's lips. "Somebody"—she narrows her eyes at Grandma Jo—"kept plying him with whiskey into the wee hours."

Grandma Jo waves a hand dismissively. "Not my fault the boy can't hold his liquor. I matched him glass for glass, and I'm right as rain."

Jimmy hides a chuckle behind his hand.

"Laugh while you can," Mom tells him. "You won't think it's funny when she tries to drink you under the table at the next family event. If there's a get-together after Enya's fight, you'll see what I mean."

He freezes, and so do I. We haven't talked about what happens beyond this weekend, other than we want to see if our relationship leads anywhere. But his expression tells me he wants to spend more time with my family. Badly. His eagerness to get to know them better should put me off since I've avoided relationships for so long, but it doesn't. Instead, it occurs to me I'd like to bring him back here in the future to show him around my hometown properly.

He clears his throat. "I can't wait."

Neither can I. I'm in over my head when it comes to Jimmy.

By the time I park outside Enya's townhouse, my face aches from smiling. The whole trip back, we just talked, and it was awesome. If there had been a sliver of doubt in my mind that Enya is the girl for me, it's gone. Regardless of whether she decides I'm the guy for her, I'm all in.

"Want to come inside?" Enya asks as she unclips her seat belt.

"Yeah." I mentally fist-pump. Earlier, we discussed our expectations. We decided we're seeing each other exclusively but aren't going to make a big deal of it, and we hope our friends follow suit.

She collects her bags from the back of the car, and I resist the urge to carry them for her because I doubt she'd appreciate the gesture, however well-meaning it might be. Her strength and capability are a source of pride, and I don't want to mess with that. I follow her to the doorstep and she passes me one of the bags while she searches in her pockets for a key. When she lets us in, the inside of the house is cozy and welcoming. It's tidy but also the sort of place where you could kick up your feet on a Friday night and relax. She wanders through the entrance to the living area and sets her bags on the ground. Her tongue flicks out and runs over her lips. Blood surges to my dick in response. Just as I'm mentally reprimanding myself for getting wound up from such a simple thing, her eyes meet mine. They burn with desire.

"Holy fuck, En." I groan. "You can't look at me like that."

She launches herself at me, and I catch her as her legs wrap around my waist. Her pussy cradles my cock as she attacks my mouth. My eyes roll back in my head, and I rock against her. She whimpers and clasps my face between her palms, kissing me with a desperation that stuns me. But then, as suddenly as it started, she stops, panting as she catches her breath.

"I'm sorry." Her head flops forward until her forehead touches mine. "I didn't mean to maul you like that. You said you want to take this slow, and I respect your boundaries. I don't know what came over me. You can put me down."

I stare at her contrite expression. It's difficult to process her words when my erection is throbbing so persistently. Am I really going to say no? And for what —to make sure she doesn't regret being with me? She's a grown woman. She can make her own decisions, and it certainly seems like she wants this.

"Fuck waiting," I decide.

Her eyes widen, but then she flashes a grin. "You want me."

"More than anything." I spread my palms over her ass cheeks, supporting her weight as I carry her to the sofa. I sit and place her on my lap. "But do you want me?"

"So damn much." She rests her hands on my chest. "This has all been such a whirlwind, but I know it's right."

"Do you have condoms?" I ask because I intentionally didn't pack any, knowing I wouldn't want to get carried away and do something hasty that would bite me in the butt.

She nods. "In the bedroom." She slips off my lap, hauls me to my feet, and drags me down the hall to a room that smells of lavender. The walls are pale blue and a massive bed dominates the space. Photo frames adorn the dresser and I scan a few, seeing many of her family members and several people I don't recognize. Friends, perhaps. They're the sort of pictures I don't have because my only friend outside the gym is Zane, and as for family… well, they're best forgotten.

"You'd better be sure about this," I warn her. "Because if I get a taste of you, I'm going to want more."

She waggles her eyebrows. "I hope we're talking about the same kind of tasting." But then she grows serious. "I'm sure."

That's all the green light I need. I yank my T-shirt off and dump it on the floor as I stalk toward her. She doesn't bend in the face of my intensity. She holds my gaze as best she can while shrugging out of her own shirt, revealing miles of gloriously bare skin. She steps forward as I reach her and threads her arms around my neck. Our mouths meet in a hungry blaze of passion. I smooth my hands up her back and shudder at the silky texture of her skin against my body. I break away from her mouth and suck her nipple through the sheer lace fabric of her bra. I can feel it bead under my tongue, and I flick the nubbin.

"Were you hoping to get lucky when you wore this?" I ask, because it's the kind of bra designed to drive a man wild.

"Yes." She arches in a way that thrusts her tits into my face.

I reach behind her and fumble with the clasp. My

fingers are clumsy with eagerness, but after a few agonizing moments, I manage to unfasten the damn thing and toss it aside.

"I was right," I breathe as I gaze at those perfect handfuls of flesh. "Dusky rose."

"Jimmy," she whines. "Hurry up."

I turn my attention to the other breast and lick it, suck it, pepper it with kisses until she's breathing heavily. I edge her toward the bed and give her a little push. As she lies back, I kick off my shoes, then my jeans. I tug off her footwear while she undoes her fly and we work together to peel down her jeans. Her panties match her bra. They barely cover her pussy, and I have them off before she can even draw breath.

I kneel over her and gaze at every curve and plane of her body. I don't have words for how beautiful she is; it's the kind of beauty that's soul deep, and even if my eyes were closed, I'd feel it with my heart.

"Perfect," I whisper.

"So are you," she replies.

I look away, unable to accept the compliment. Nothing about me is perfect. I'm a trailer park kid with a chip on his shoulder. She's a world-famous athlete adored by half the nation.

"Jimmy." She reaches for my hand and holds it firmly. "You are. I don't care how many times I have to say it, I will until you accept it's the truth."

I meet her eyes, and the emotion in them blows me away. "I—"

I don't know what to say, and she seems to sense that because she reaches for the waistband of my boxers. "Shh. Just feel. Okay?"

I nod, relieved. When we're both naked, I stretch alongside her and brush my lips against hers while I slick a finger through the folds of her pussy. She's hot and wet to touch, and she shivers as I stroke her. My dick wants to be inside that wet heat so bad it hurts. Precum drips from the flushed head.

"I want you in me," Enya says, moving her hips restlessly. "We can go slowly after. Please, just fuck me."

I kiss her again. "Condom?"

She gestures to the dresser. I reach for the handle, pausing to check with her before opening it. She nods. The box of condoms is near the top but unopened, which selfishly pleases me. I hurry to get suited up and settle between her thighs. I ease into her. Fuck, she's tight. I throw my head back and plead with my dick to hang in there long enough to make her come. When I'm certain I've got myself under control, I kiss her until she can't stay still anymore, rubbing herself against me and mewling in pleasure.

My palms on either side of her, I rise up and look at where we're joined, watching my flesh fuck in and out of her. Each time I go deep, her channel tightens around me as though trying to keep me there. I groan at the sight. So fucking hot.

"Baby, you feel like you were made for me."

She reaches for my face and drags me into another kiss. My arms give out, and I land on her. I worry for a moment that I've hurt her, but then she screams, and it has nothing to do with pain. Well, damn. She likes it rough.

I rear back, grab her thighs, and shove into her over and over again. She moans and whimpers. Then, right as my balls draw up and I'm afraid I might blow my load, she goes tense and releases a keening cry.

"Oh fuck. Fuck. Fuck." Colors explode behind my eyes as I come. I open my mouth, ready to spill all kinds of words about love and forever, but thankfully manage to snap it shut before I do. I ride out the wave, and once it's settled, I lean forward and brush Enya's hair away from her face. I kiss her forehead, her cheeks, the tip of her nose, and finally, her mouth. I can't tell her I love her yet. It would send her running for the hills. But I can hold her close and show her how things could be between us.

"Stay?" she asks softly.

Hope flares in my chest. "For as long as you want me."

7

Over the next two weeks, Jimmy and I spend a lot of time together. Training, chilling, getting naked. *Lots* of getting naked. But every time I have to go for a run, lift weights, or put in some extra hours at the gym, I get this little niggle of doubt. It's like I'm waiting for him to grow tired of my busy life, which is crazy since his is busy too, but it's been a bone of contention in most of my relationships, and I just can't get my head around the fact he honestly doesn't seem to care.

Today, everything is about to come to a head. We've been planning to jump from the Stratosphere Hotel together this afternoon, but I've just gotten off the phone with Seth, who's asked me to come to the gym. My big fight is fast approaching, and he'd arranged for me to have a one-on-one training session with Maryse De Vries, the Dutch former world champion and someone who's previously defeated my British opponent, next week. Unfortunately, Maryse has been called out of the country and her flight leaves tonight, which means if I want to see her, it has to be this afternoon.

Jimmy has been looking forward to the jump all week. So have I, for that matter. I hate that I'll be letting him down. But this is a one-off opportunity. Maryse might have the advice I need to win my last-chance fight. I wipe a hand down my face and groan. I'm going to have to cancel. Better get this over with.

I find Jimmy in the kitchen. He's just come from the stationary cycle, so his T-shirt is plastered to his tightly-honed body. I bite my lip and take a moment to appreciate the sight. He fills a glass of water and passes it to me, one side of his mouth hitching up in a way that lets me know he's noticed me checking him out.

"What did Seth want?" he asks.

Ugh. That.

I wring my hands. "I'm really sorry to do this, but I need to postpone the Stratosphere jump. He asked me to come in this afternoon for the session with Maryse De Vries. She's had to reschedule and won't be able to do next week."

He looks disappointed but nods. "That's okay. We can do the jump another time. Maybe after your fight?"

That's it? Surely not.

I frown. "You can go without me if you'd like."

He shoots me a pointed look. "Half the fun is doing it with you. We can wait a couple of weeks. It's no big deal."

My back teeth grind together. He says that, but does he really mean it? One of my exes used to say something similar, but then he'd sulk or turn passive-aggressive about it later. I can't read Jimmy, and while he doesn't seem the sort to do that, I don't know for sure. I'm afraid this is going to come back and kick me in the ass.

"Seriously?" I demand. "That's it? No big deal?"

"Yeah." He sips his water and leans against the counter. "It's a shame, but it is what it is. We'll get back to it soon enough."

"Come on." My tone is full of disbelief. "You must be annoyed. I'm being a flake."

He sets his glass on the counter and places a hand on each of my shoulders. "Enya, you're not being a flake. Sometimes you have to prioritize your career over other things." His blue eyes bore into mine. "I don't hold your career against you, and I hope in the future, you won't hold mine against me."

"Of course not," I mutter as it finally begins to sink in. He's not burying his resentment. He's actually okay with this.

"Besides, I wouldn't mind coming along to meet Maryse, if that's okay with you." He grins mischievously. "She's a legend."

I swat him playfully. "You can come. But don't hog her attention. She's all mine."

"Got it." He winks and my heart gives an extra thud. He's so damn tempting.

"I want to kiss you," I tell him.

His hands shift down to my hips. "Then do it."

I do. And we don't stop at a kiss.

JIMMY

Today is Enya's rest day, and I'm taking advantage of it to introduce her to the one person from my past who means anything to me. My best friend, Zane. We stopped being roommates the moment we could each afford to have our own place, but we still live within the same apartment block.

Enya's hand is in mine as I lead her to the door. I can sense she's nervous. She knows Zane is important to me, and I think she's worried about impressing him. I'm not concerned, though. Zane will love her. I grin, imagining his face when he sees us. I told him I'm bringing my new girlfriend over, but I didn't mention her name.

I stop outside his apartment and knock. The door opens immediately, and Zane catches my eye, wearing a shit-eating grin. He turns to Enya, and his jaw practically hits the floor.

"Fuck," he exclaims, his gaze pinging from her to me and back again. "Holy shit. You're Enya Sears."

Enya glares at me. "You didn't tell him?"

I chuckle as Zane's face turns red. "I didn't want to ruin the moment."

"Men," she mutters, then turns her thousand-megawatt smile on Zane.

"You must be pranking me." Zane glances around as though waiting for people to jump out and start laughing. "You can't really be dating this knucklehead."

"Hey," I protest.

Enya sighs. "Right now, I'm wondering about my life choices, but yes, I'm actually dating this knucklehead."

"Whoa, whoa." I hold up my hands. "You two aren't supposed to gang up on me."

Zane seems to be coming around because he winks at her. "Why don't you and I get to know each other better and leave him in the corridor so he has time to think about what he's done?"

"That sounds perfect." She follows him inside. He flicks the door at me when I try to join them, but not very hard. I catch it and step through, closing it behind me. Like my place, Zane's is tidy, but unlike mine, he has personal knickknacks on every surface. He says he likes how they look, but I think it's his way of marking his territory—something neither of us got to do when we were younger.

"Can I get you a drink?" he asks as Enya and I settle on a sofa in the living room.

"Just some water, please," she replies.

He returns a few minutes later and sets down a platter with a glass of water, a mug of coffee, and a cup of peppermint tea. He passes Enya the water, sets the coffee on a coaster in front of me, and takes the tea for himself.

"So," he says, still looking at her as though he expects her to disappear at any moment. "Has he told you about the crazy crush he had on you when we were in high school?"

"No." She raises an eyebrow at me. "But now I need to know."

My cheeks flood with heat. "Asshole," I mutter half-heartedly, but I'd already accepted I wouldn't get out of this meeting unscathed.

"Our boy Jimmy"— he pauses for dramatic effect— "saw you fight when he was seventeen and decided right then and there that you were his perfect woman."

I bury my flaming face in my palms. "It wasn't quite like that."

Zane snickers. "Yes, it was. If you'd been able to, you'd have had a poster of her on your wall."

Okay, so that part is true.

"Jimmy?" Enya lays a hand on my forearm, her tone gentle.

"Yeah," I admit, raising my face from my palms. "I

probably would have. But can you blame me? You're a fucking goddess in the cage."

Now it's her turn to blush. "I don't try to be."

"I know," I groan. "It's effortless. It's just who you are."

She smiles teasingly. "It's pretty adorable that you had a crush on me."

"Adorable." I glare at Zane. "Now look what you've done."

He leans forward, arms resting on his thighs, and pays me no attention. "I've got all the goods on Jimmy. Just tell me what you want to know."

Two hours later, when we return to my apartment, I feel like I've been put through the wringer.

"Isn't he supposed to interrogate you about your intentions, not throw me under the bus a zillion times?" I complain as I flop onto the bed.

Enya sprawls beside me and props her head on her hand. "I think I prefer it this way. Now I know where to go if I ever need Jimmy-related gossip."

"He's such a traitor." I'm going to do the exact same thing when he finally introduces me to a partner.

She sticks out her tongue, but then her expression grows serious. "I have a question for you."

"Anything. What is it?"

She breathes in, then slowly lets it out. "Do you see me as more than just the girl you used to have a crush on, or is this relationship based on some kind of fantasy you had about finally bagging 'Enya Sears?'" She puts her name in finger quotation marks as though trying to divorce who she is as a person from her public persona.

My heart drops. I can understand why she's asking, but I hate that she doubts me for even a second. I sit up and reach for her hand. "Look, I won't deny that I was embarrassingly hung up on you before I even met you, but I haven't spent the past two weeks with some fantasy girl. I've spent it with *you*. I moved on from my celebrity crush ages ago, but when I met you, I felt something all over again. It was real, based on who you are in here." I tap her chest with my free hand. "I swear it." I lean down and brush my lips over hers. "You're fun. And being around you makes me happy. Do you believe me?"

Her lips curl into the most beautiful smile I've ever seen. "I do. Thanks for bearing with me. I just had to ask."

I nod. "I get it." In her shoes, I'd wonder the same thing. "But I hope you don't mind me saying that I think teenage Jimmy was on to something when he chose you as his fantasy girl."

"He sounds like a smart guy." Her smile turns mischievous. "What would he think if you told him that one day Enya Sears would give him a blow job?"

I snort. "He'd lose his mind."

She rolls on top of me, grabs my waistband and tugs it down. My dick comes to attention, ready to obey her every command. She frees it from the confines of my underwear and touches the tip of her tongue to the domed head. My hips punch forward, desperate to get inside her by whatever means possible.

"Tut tut." She pulls away and palms my balls. "I'm in charge."

"Fine," I grit out. "Please suck me."

"Hmm." She draws me into her mouth and I clench my fists, fighting the need to come. "Like this?" The words are muffled by my dick, and I force myself to lie still so she doesn't stop. Her tongue curls around me and slides up and down my length. She holds my gaze as her cheeks hollow out. It feels fucking incredible.

"Oh God."

She uses one hand to play with my balls while the other grips the part of my dick her mouth can't reach. I stare at her, slack-jawed and panting. She's the most erotic thing I've seen in my life. Suddenly, she goes deep, and I grab handfuls of the blankets because the alternative is to clutch her hair. She hums around me and then releases her grip on my balls so she can play with her pussy.

"Baby, that's so hot," I gasp. "So fucking sexy."

She moans. A shudder racks my body, and I barely manage to sputter a warning before I come. She swallows every drop and continues licking me as I twitch through aftershocks. I haul her up my body and kiss her. She tastes of my cum, and a savage possessiveness roars through me, giving me a second wind. I roll her onto her back and yank her shorts down. She's going commando beneath and her pussy glistens. Damn, she's beautiful.

"I'm going to make you scream."

I deploy every trick I ever learned with my tongue until she's as replete and satisfied as I am.

Teenage Jimmy would never fucking believe it.

8

I bump fists with Harley at the end of a gentle round of sparring and nod toward the bathroom. "I'll be back in a moment."

I slip my padded knuckle covers off and stride toward the ladies' room, but then slow as I approach because there's a strange noise coming from within. It sounds like crying. I drop my knuckle covers on the ground and step inside, hesitantly scanning the row of cubicles. The first one on the left is closed. I pause in front of it, wondering whether it's a good idea to interrupt. The only other women who've been here today are Ashlin and Tempe. I hate the thought of either of them sobbing inside a toilet cubicle, but I also don't want to embarrass them by witnessing something they'd rather keep private. A hiccupping sob makes up my mind for me. Whoever is in there, they need support. I knock softly, and the noise dies.

"You okay?" I ask, then mentally kick myself because, clearly, she's not.

"Enya?"

My heart squeezes. It's Tempe. "Yeah, it's me. Is there anything I can do to help?"

She's quiet for a moment, then I hear the latch click and the door opens a couple of inches. Tempe's face appears in the gap. Her bloodshot eyes blink at me, and mine prickle in response because I'm a sympathetic crier. "Is it just you?"

I nod. "What's wrong?"

She opens the door all the way and swipes at the tears trickling down her cheeks. "Can I have a hug?"

"Oh, honey. Of course." I pull her into an embrace and hold her tightly, ignoring the way her body begins to shake as her sobs start anew. I smooth a hand down her back as her tears soak the shoulder of my tank top. "I'm here for you."

We stay like that for so long I'm surprised Harley doesn't come to check on me. Eventually, Tempe pulls back and takes a few purposeful breaths.

"Chad broke up with me," she says when she has herself under control.

"I'm so sorry." After what she said about their sex life, I thought something must be wrong, but I'd never have guessed they were about to call it quits. "Did it happen today?"

She nods and presses her lips together, as if to prevent more tears from falling. "It's been coming for a long time, but I guess my head was in the sand. I thought if I pretended that we'd get past our problems, then maybe we would." She whimpers. "One day I might be able to look back and be glad he ended it, but right now, it hurts too much."

I wrap my arms around her again. "He's an idiot and he's going to regret letting you go."

I feel her head move as she shakes it. "He won't," she whispers. "He's been upset about the number of hours I put into training for a while now. Back at my old gym, the coaches didn't take me seriously, so I guess he thought I'd never get anywhere and that I'd quit soon and give him a few children. But now that I've gone pro, he's had to face up to what it means to be with an athlete. He's asked me several times to cut back, but I just can't. Even if I could work something out with Seth, I wouldn't want to. I love being here. This is what I want to do with my life." Her expression crumples. "I wish he could accept that."

Her words bounce around my mind like an echo chamber. They sound so much like the conversations I've had with my exes. Like the ones I'm afraid will happen with Jimmy.

"He's a douche," I tell her. "If he doesn't want you happy—even if it means less time with him—then he doesn't deserve you." Even as I say it, I can't help but think about what a difficult time I have internalizing that message myself. I thought I'd finally convinced myself Jimmy is here to stay, but Tempe's heartbreak is stirring all the emotions I'd rather not deal with. All the pain from the times I've been through something similar. The resignation of knowing that maybe love just isn't on the horizon for me. And then the tender thread of hope that maybe things can change. I'm going to hold onto that thread with everything I have.

She withdraws from my embrace and sighs. "I've tried to tell myself that, but it doesn't work. Logically, I know it, but my heart doesn't give a fuck about logic."

Tell me about it.

"I know where you're coming from." I take her hand and squeeze it. "Consider the breakup a rite of passage. I've had a couple of boyfriends dump me because of my training hours."

"You have?" She looks like she can't decide whether

to be relieved or horrified. "But there must be guys out there who understand, right?"

"Absolutely." I sound more certain than I am.

She flashes a sad smile. "You're so lucky to have Jimmy. He'll never give you a hard time about stuff like that."

Something inside me settles. I know she's right. I just *know* it. And I just have to trust him.

Tempe glances at the door when the guys in the gym break into raucous laughter, Devon's voice rising above them all.

"Typical Dev." She shakes her head. "Now there's a devoted boyfriend. Hmph. Maybe I need to find a fighter. It seems to be working well for you and Harley."

"Go on, then," I encourage. "But give yourself time to recover first—and stay away from *my* fighter."

She lets out a watery laugh. "Don't worry. Jimmy isn't my type. Besides, he's so crazy about you, I don't think he even knows other women exist."

I grin, feeling lighter. "Yeah, he's pretty great." I take a couple steps toward the exit and tug her hand. "Come on. You need to punch the crap out of something."

Jimmy

The weeks have raced by, and there are only a few days left until Enya's fight against the British champion. My girl is in great shape, and I've been making sure she has food ready when she needs it and gets to bed at a reasonable time. I've also been wearing her out so she gets a great sleep. 'Cause I'm just a good guy like that.

This evening, I've organized a get-together at her place. I'm hoping she doesn't mind, but I want to do something to show her how much support she has and to help get her head in the game. It's after five now, so Seth should be finishing up his one-on-one session with her—the last hard training effort before the fight. Meanwhile, I've cooked enough to feed a small army. Fighters have slowly been rocking up to her house for the past half hour. Enya let me know where the spare key was, and I'm hoping she doesn't mind me using it this way. I'm more than happy to kick everyone out if she wants quiet time.

"Hey, man." Jase claps me on the shoulder as he steps through the front door. His partner, Lena, is close behind him. She smiles and greets me. I nod to her.

Gabe follows and passes me a bowl of salad. "From Sydney."

"Tell her thanks." His girlfriend is scheduled to work at the hospital tonight, so she can't be here. It's nice of her to make a contribution anyway. I take the salad to the kitchen and return to the living room with a cooler containing a selection of drinks—including water, which is all Enya should be drinking at the moment. More than ten people are crammed into the space—which seemed open and airy up until it was stuffed to the brim with fighters. Tempe, Leo, Camile, Tony, and Enya's other City Fight Center friends are piled onto one sofa and the beanbag in front of it, while Jase, Lena, Gabe, Harley, Devon, and Ashlin occupy another sofa and a couple of armchairs. Ashlin's hand rests protectively on her rounded stomach. There's one space, right in front of the large screen television, left open for Enya. I'm not sure where I'll fit, but I'll figure something out. There's always the floor.

"I've got it cued up to play her opponent's most recent fight," Leo says. "Are you sure we're not going to overwhelm her? She can get pretty sensitive about pre-fight rituals considering her track record."

"I'm 90 percent sure she'll be happy," I reply. "But on the off-chance I'm wrong, you'll all just have to clear out quickly, with no hard feelings. That okay?"

He nods. Nerves zap around my stomach. Leo has known Enya for longer than me and he's worried. I hope I haven't read this situation wrong, but from what I've come to know about her, I think she needs to see how many people believe she can win.

A car door slams outside and we all freeze. Everybody invited has arrived other than Enya and Seth, which means the guest of honor is here.

"Everyone be quiet," I hiss, then turn off the light and hurry to the front door. I hope they all parked around the corner as I asked so she won't have seen the cars and been clued in to the fact something is happening.

I open the door just as she reaches it. Her lips part and her eyes widen in surprise. She must have showered at the gym because her hair is damp and curls loosely around her shoulders. She's changed out of her exercise gear and into a blouse and cutoff shorts. I kiss her and the scent of her berry-flavored body wash wafts over me. Closing my eyes, I pray not to pitch a tent in my jeans. We've done some dirty, dirty things with that body wash.

"I wasn't expecting you," she says, fiddling with the strap of the duffel bag that's over her shoulder.

"How did your last official training session go?"

She smiles. "Really good. I'm feeling positive about Saturday."

"That's great." Hopefully she'll feel even more confident in a few hours. I reach down and lace my fingers through hers. "I made dinner."

Right on cue, her stomach grumbles. She laughs. "I hope it isn't anything too heavy. I feel like fresh salad and maybe some chicken."

"You're in luck." Instead of taking her to the kitchen, I lead her to the living room and switch on the light, impressed nobody has made a noise yet.

The moment the room lights up, a chorus of "Surprise!" rings out.

Enya stumbles back a step, her hand fluttering over her heart. "Holy crap! You scared the life out of me."

"Sorry," I murmur, and a bunch of her contrite friends do the same.

Enya moves further into the room, gazing around at the food on the table, the training buddies taking up every inch of free space, and the video on the TV. "What's all this?"

"We're here to help with the game plan." The rumbling voice comes from behind her. Seth is standing in the doorway. He must have rushed over from the gym as soon as she left. His eyes quickly seek out Ashlin before returning to Enya. "You've worked really hard the past few months, and the whole team is behind you. We're here to show our support and to reinforce the best strategies for your fight this weekend."

"Oh my God." Her tone is soft and full of wonder as she turns to me. I mentally pump a fist. *I didn't screw up.* "Did you organize this?"

"Yeah. But everyone wants to be here. Just like

we're all going to be there this weekend to watch you kick ass."

"Thank you." She grabs me by the shirt and pulls me close, then presses her mouth to mine. I revel in the taste that's become my new addiction, but before things become too heated, she draws back. "I can't believe you'd do this for me."

I feel my cheeks flush, knowing everyone is watching, but I'm all in with her, and I won't shy away from letting her know it. "I have complete faith in you, and these guys do too. You're going to rock it."

She kisses me again, so briefly I have the urge to grab her and demand more, but I resist. She gestures to the spot in the center of the room. "Sit with me?"

"There's only room for one."

She rolls her eyes. "I want to sit on my boyfriend's lap. Is that okay with you?"

"Oh." My flush deepens. *Idiot.* "Fuck yes. As long as you don't mind him being a moron sometimes."

She pats my cheek. "That just makes him cuter. I'll always want him."

My heart seizes.

I'll always want him.

God, I hope that's true. I've all but served myself up on a silver platter. If she changes her mind, it'll tear me apart.

I sit on the sofa. She gathers a plate of food and perches on my lap. Leo starts the fight, and as we all shift our focus to the action on the screen, I make a silent wish for us to have many more nights like this to come.

9

Enya

I'm pacing barefoot through my house, wrapped in a soft robe, when I hear Jimmy's voice coming from the spare bedroom. I pause outside. The door is open, and he's standing in front of the window, one hand propped on his hip, the other holding a phone to his ear. I can't see his face, but the tone of his voice makes it clear he's frustrated.

"I can't do tonight, Brian."

I frown. Brian is his manager. An older guy who isn't exactly the cream of the crop as far as managers go, but he seems to have done reasonably well for Jimmy.

"You know why." He drops his hand from his hip and rakes it through his hair. "Enya is fighting."

At that, nerves creep into the pit of my stomach. With twelve hours to go before I face off in an intercontinental battle, I've been trying not to dwell on what might happen. Promoters keep giving me big opportunities, and I consistently fall short. Second isn't good enough this time; I worry the opportunities will dry up if I don't win. Logically, I know losing this fight won't mean the end of my career, but it would be a massive blow.

"Yeah, I know I won't get a chance like this often," he says. I walk over and touch his arm so he knows I'm there. He smiles down at me and speaks to Brian again. "Can I have a couple of hours to think about it?" He waits for a response. "Great. Thanks. I appreciate the work you've put in on this." He nods as Brian says something. "Okay, talk soon." Then he hangs up.

"What was that about?" I ask.

He slips his phone into his pocket and brushes a kiss over my mouth. "Samson & Sons Sportswear are having a meet and greet with athletes they're interested in sponsoring. They had an MMA fighter pull out, and Brian scored me an invitation to fill the gap." Excitement sparkles in his eyes.

"That's incredible!" I leap into his arms and hug him tightly. When he returns the embrace, I breathe in his scent, and it soothes my nerves. I pull back. "Samson are massive. Partnering with them could be a turning point for your career." I'm so pleased for him. He's spent weeks supporting me whole-heartedly, and it's wonderful to be able to do the same for him. But then my grin fades as I recall his conversation and realize what it means. "It's tonight, isn't it?"

"Yeah." His expression is pained. "It's not far from the event venue, but it runs during the time of your fight."

I try not to let my disappointment show. This is the biggest sponsorship opportunity he's ever had, and I can see how much he wants it. It would be selfish of me to stand in the way, no matter how much I want him in my corner tonight. Asking him to give up this chance would be the equivalent of my exes urging me to let go of my dreams.

"You should go," I tell him. "Samson are a big deal. If you miss out, you'll kick yourself for it later."

He sighs and pinches the bridge of his nose. "You've trained really hard, and I want to be there for you when you win."

When. I love how he says that. He has more faith in me than I do. He's a good person, and that's why I need to step aside no matter how much I hate coming in second place—whether it's in the cage or in a tug-of-war between our relationship and Jimmy's career. Honestly, I can't imagine I'll ever win that one. He's just as ambitious as I was several years ago, and I'd never have put a man above my career. If I'd known any women who did, I'd have told them they were an idiot. Because of that, I won't put him in the position of having to choose. Especially not when he's fought so hard to get to where he is.

"You can celebrate with me afterward." I do my best to smile, but he isn't fooled. I take his hand and soften my voice. "My family will be there. I won't be alone. Do it, Jimmy. I don't want to be the reason you miss out. You'd resent me."

He draws me to his chest and rests his cheek on the top of my head. I wallow in the sensation of being held by him. "I could never resent you."

"Of course you could." I back away and head for the door. "I'm going for a walk. I need to get in the right headspace for tonight." I'm not supposed to exercise the day of a fight, except for a warm-up at the venue, but walking never hurt anyone.

"I'll come." He starts forward, but I stop him with a shake of my head.

"I'd rather be alone." I wince when his face falls.

"I'm sorry, I just need some quiet to get my thoughts in order." I can see it's on the tip of his tongue to say he's capable of being quiet, but he holds the words back, and I'm grateful for that. "Promise you'll take the time to think through your decision carefully?"

He frowns and gives me a dark, unreadable look, but then nods. "Fine, I'll think about it."

"Good." My shoulders slump and I force a smile to hide the tears gathering in my eyes. This is the right thing to do. I can't have him throw away his hard work for my sake. "Because if you're at the venue tonight when you should be meeting with Samson, we're going to have a problem."

He doesn't speak, nod, or shake his head. He just turns away. Somehow, that's even worse. I retreat to my bedroom, dress, and leave without seeking him out again. But when my trainers hit the pavement, I can't help wishing he'd argued. I'm such a hypocrite.

Get your shit together, Sears. This is what you want.

At least, I think it is.

JIMMY

I take the hottest shower I can handle while I think about my options. On one hand, a company with enough money to bankroll me for years has invited me to an exclusive event, the likes of which I've never attended before. I'm amazed the people running Samson & Sons Sportswear know I exist, let alone want to meet me. If I make a good impression, it would be another step further from the trailer park. My main goal in life has been to put as much distance between me and my past as possible, and to make it so I'll never have to go back. With that in mind, it should be a no-brainer. But it isn't. Not by a long shot. Because while my MMA career has been the driving force between almost all of my decisions, it isn't my only dream.

I rinse soap out of my hair and rest my forehead against the wall, letting the water drum onto my back. Enya's place has amazing water pressure. Presumably it's been designed to maximize her muscle recovery. Which brings me to my other dream: Enya. I never imagined I'd have a chance with her, but now that I do, I don't want to let her down. She's an amazing woman, and being with her has made me happier than anything else—including MMA. Hell, knowing I can come home to her at the end of the day is a better feeling than the first time I earned a paycheck all on my own and didn't have to split it with my deadbeat parents.

I growl in frustration and shut off the water. I feel like I'm being backed into a corner, forced to choose between two dreams, and while I know it's not as black and white as that, it's difficult to convince my subconscious. I towel dry and dress in a pair of shorts and a T-shirt, then I grab my wallet and pull out the photograph I keep in the coin pocket. Usually, seeing the broken-down trailer is enough to spur me into whatever action puts it more firmly in my rearview mirror, but not today.

What the hell am I supposed to do?

I wait for Enya to return, but when she does, she doesn't seem interested in discussing the matter further. She brushes aside my concern and starts getting ready for the event. Frustrated, I find a quiet corner and call Brian. I'm not even sure what to say, but when he answers, I find the words spilling from my lips without any forethought. At the end of the conversation, I calmly set the phone down and head for the sofa. My mind whirls with the potential implications of what I've done, but I don't have any regret. I'm at peace with the decision I've made, but I hope it won't come back to bite me in the ass.

10

Enya

I stand in the corridor, listening to the crowd in the arena as my opponent precedes me to the cage. The energy level is high. They've been pumped up by the fights so far, but mine is the penultimate event. The guy ahead gestures for us to move to the entryway. I take a few steps forward and stop just out of sight of the audience.

Seth places a hand on my shoulder. "You've got this."

I nod because I can't find the words to agree. I've trained with the best and been taught by the best, but that means nothing if I don't have heart.

Big heart, heavy hands, killer kicks. Make her submit.

I silently repeat the mantra to myself.

Suddenly, there's a noise behind us. I turn and find Jimmy standing with Harley and Seth. My eyes widen. He's *here*?

When he didn't turn up earlier, I assumed he'd done the sensible thing and gone to mingle with his potential sponsor. Had I gotten it wrong?

"You're here," I whisper.

"I wouldn't miss this for anything." His voice is firm. Certain.

I search his eyes—looking for what, I don't know. The emotion I see in them steals my breath. I raise my chin. "Thank you."

I'm not sure he's made the best decision for himself, but still, he decided to be here for me—even when I didn't ask him to—and that means something.

He comes closer and cups my face between his palms. "I will always choose you."

"But where have you been?"

He grins. "Hanging out with your family. I helped Kelsey with her supporter signs."

I press a fist to my mouth to stifle a laugh. "Please tell me they're not glittery."

My family flew into the city earlier today, but I haven't seen them because I wanted to avoid anything that might get me out of the zone—which my crazy family are certainly capable of doing. He must have called them and arranged to meet up while I was busy avoiding him.

His grin stretches. "Oh, they are. One hundred percent. Nothing I could say would change her mind."

I shake my head. "God, I love you."

His jaw drops. I just blink at him, stunned by my own confession. This is totally not the right time.

"Seriously?" he asks.

"Yes," I say, because it's the truth. "I know it's fast. Maybe I'm crazy, but everything about us feels right."

His eyes are suspiciously shiny. "I've loved you for what feels like forever." He pays no attention to our audience. "I've got your back, baby."

"I know." We embrace tightly, and then he releases

me as the announcer calls my name from the arena. "I'd better go."

He steps back. "You have this."

I do. I *so* do.

I adjust my stance and refocus on the door in front of me. My music plays and I stride forward, emerging into the spacious main section of the venue. The crowd goes wild. I lift a hand to acknowledge them and then focus on the cage and the stocky woman pacing within it. My opponent tonight is shorter than me but more muscular. If I'd been facing off against her a few months ago, I'd have been intimidated by that, but my own body is stronger than ever, and I know I can match her.

I pause at the base of the cage while someone checks my mouthguard and gloves, then I bound up the stairs and pump my fists above my head. Energy flows through my body. I hear someone scream my name, but I don't look in their direction. I head to my corner and wait for the referee to summon us to the center. He gives the usual spiel and then I bump fists with my opponent. She tries to stare me down and I hold her gaze, not even looking away as we back up. The round begins, and we launch into motion.

She flies at me, fist first. I dart out of the way and retaliate with a leg kick. She charges again, and I use a push kick to keep her at a distance. She pauses the full-frontal attack, and we circle each other. After a few moments, she lunges forward to throw another punch. I raise my leg to ward her off, but instead of using her fists, she sweeps my standing leg out from under me and I hit the ground with a thud. A second later, she's on me. She pins me down and lands a couple of strikes to my face before I have the chance to cover it. We roll, using our legs and hips to battle for dominance. I come from a strong Jiu-Jitsu background, but it's difficult to get the upper hand when she's had the advantage from the moment we took the fight to the floor.

A loud beep signals the end of the round, and we each clamber to our feet before heading for our respective coaches. I try to regulate my breathing, sucking in a long, slow breath before holding it for a moment and releasing. I take stock of my injuries. My face throbs, but other than that, I'm in pretty good shape.

Someone behind me presses an ice pack to the cheek that received those first unguarded punches. Seth offers me a drink then mops the sweat from my forehead. "I'm going to give it to you straight. You got off to a good start, but you're down on points. You need to make sure you come out of this round on top." He grasps my shoulders and looks me in the eye. "You can do this, Enya. I know it, you know it, and all those people out there know it too. But remember what Maryse said? If you want it, you've gotta fight for it with everything in you, 'cause nobody is just gonna give it to you."

"I will." I feel the air move behind me, and the ice pack is removed from my face.

"I believe in you, baby," Jimmy whispers near my ear. "Show them what you've got. You're the most badass woman here, and I love you."

I turn and see the truth in his eyes. I straighten my spine. My man chose to be here with me tonight, and I'm going to make him proud. "I love you too."

"Seconds out!" the referee yells.

Jimmy brushes a kiss to my forehead, and he and Seth leave the cage. The referee summons us to him. We bump fists and the round begins. This time, I hold nothing back. If my opponent wants to go to the ground, then that's what we'll do. I can beat her there as easily as I can standing. I take her down, and we roll together. At first, I have the upper hand, but she's both strong and skilled, and before long, she's reversed our positions. I lever my feet and flip her. She tries to maintain the momentum, but I curl my arm around her neck in a chokehold. She bucks but I don't budge. Every muscle in my body is rigid, and even though I'm growing weary, I hold her in place. She can't last forever. The big win is in sight, and I will not let it slip away. Not this time.

Finally, her hand reaches out to the side, and she taps the mat. I wait for a moment until the referee acknowledges it, and then I release her. I scramble to my feet, but she stays on the ground, presumably waiting for blood flow to return. When she starts to move, I offer her a hand. She stares at it for a second, then grabs it and lets me pull her to her feet.

"Thanks." I haul her into a one-armed embrace.

"Good fight," she replies.

I head to my corner, where the beaming faces of my crew remind me of one very important fact: I *won*.

"You did it!" Seth high-fives me and pulls me into a fierce embrace. "I'm so proud of you."

I hug him back, my brain still having a hard time accepting what happened. "You got me here," I tell him. "This is *our* win."

"You did the hard part."

He releases me and then I'm being yanked into another strong pair of arms. *Jimmy's.* He peppers my face with kisses, moving softly over the area that's already bruising.

"That was fucking incredible." He grins at me as though I'm the most amazing thing he's ever seen. It warms me from the inside, soothing the parts of my body that ache or feel restless. "Baby, you just beat the British champion."

"I did, didn't I?" I murmur in wonder. Then it hits me all at once. I bury my face in his chest as happy tears stream down my cheeks. "Finally. I won."

"Yeah, you did."

The referee summons both fighters to the center of the cage. I have a fat lip and one of my eyes is swelling shut, but I barely notice as he announces me the winner. I'm handed a massive trophy by a former women's champion who I've idolized forever but have hardly spoken to.

She winks. "You deserve it."

Oh my God.

"I used to have a poster of you on my wall," I blurt.

Beside me, my opponent laughs. "So did I," she adds in a British accent.

I smile over at her, and she smiles back. Despite her loss, I wonder if we might become friends. I'll have to make a point to talk to her later.

We separate as the official part of the fight ends. I shake hands with each team member from the opposing side and then exit the cage and leap into Jimmy's arms. Thousands of people cheer as he, Seth, Harley, and I retreat to the back rooms. When Jimmy sets me on my feet, I grab Harley and hug the crap out of her. She's stiff for a moment—not usually one for displays of affection—but then softens and hugs me back.

"Celebration at my place later," I announce as the rest of the team swarm us. "My family have organized a party." I'm hugged, high-fived, and congratulated to within an inch of my life, and people promise to come by later.

As soon as I get a few seconds to breathe, I find

Jimmy and thread my fingers through his. The next fifteen minutes are a blur, but I don't let him go, and finally, by some miracle, we end up alone.

"I'm still buzzing," I tell him, pressing the length of my body to his. Adrenaline is a godsend in a lot of ways, but it leaves me jittery.

"What can I do to help?" he asks.

I place my lips beside his ear. "Fuck me." I crave it so badly, my voice wobbles. "Make me come."

He scans my face. "But you're hurt, and your family are waiting."

"I can hardly feel a thing, and my family can wait a bit longer because if you don't fuck me, I'm definitely going to be hurt."

His lips curve. "We can't have that."

<hr>

Jimmy

My sexy-as-fuck woman wants me to bang her in the locker room? I can do that. Hell, after the performance she put in, I'll give her anything she wants. Seeing her out there was like watching that fight when I was a teenager all over again, except this time, I'm able to do something about my insane desire for her. I lock the door, and suddenly, the way Jase smirked and told me to make the most of it before ushering the others into the corridor makes sense. He must have known what we'd end up doing. He's probably done the same damn thing.

"It's going to be quick," I warn, since I don't want anyone interrupting us.

She gives me a meaningful look. "I'm wound up, Jimmy. I never thought it'd last long."

Well, okay then.

I cup her cheeks and kiss her softly. Her lips are swollen, and I don't want to hurt her, but she increases the pressure and rubs herself against me.

"More," she demands. "I can take it."

I back her against the wall as she fumbles with the fly of my jeans. I push her hands aside and undo them myself, then shove them over my hips. She shimmies her shorts down and stares at me, her eyes glazed, lips parted. She's the hottest fucking thing I've ever seen. And that's before I notice her fingers are buried in her pussy.

"Fuck," I curse. "Yes, touch yourself like that, baby. Make yourself feel good."

She lets out a sob and reaches for me. "I need you. Please."

I gather her in my arms and take her weight. She wraps her legs around my waist, and my eyes roll back as she rubs the seam of her pussy over my dick. "I've got you."

I grab a condom from my pocket and work it on. Then, with one thrust, I enter her tight, hot body. I settle deep inside her and close my eyes, resting my forehead against hers. I know instinctively this is where I belong. Enya is mine and I'm hers, and that's the way it's always going to be.

My lips hover over hers. "I love you."

She shifts her hips, seeking more. "I love you too, but I'd love you forever if you'd get a move on."

I laugh, and tenderness wells within me. I'm so glad I've ended up with a woman who makes me laugh even as she makes my soul sing. Once I'm sure she's positioned comfortably, I piston in and out of her. The slick drag of her sex against mine draws a moan from me. I watch her face as I fuck into her. She's so expressive, and every bit of pleasure she's feeling shows. My jaw tightens. I'm riding the edge. My balls draw up to my body as she whimpers and mewls. I reach between us and thumb her clit. Her back arches and she opens her mouth to cry out, but I swallow the sound. I hold her as she shudders in my arms, and then, when she's limp and sated, I let myself go. A few frenzied thrusts and I shoot inside her, murmuring her name against her skin. Eventually, I have to put her down.

"Wow." She grabs a cloth to clean herself up. "We should do that after every fight."

I wipe myself off and then kiss her cheek. "I'm definitely up for starting a new tradition."

When we're both dressed and no longer smelling of sex, we head out to join the others. The last fight has finished, so people mill around the arena, chatting and mingling. I spot Seth in the crowd, speaking to Martha and Edwin, and I lace my fingers with Enya's as we make our way to them. We're only a few yards off when a man in a suit steps in front of us. At first, I try to move around him, but he holds up a hand to indicate he wants to talk. Frowning, I study him. He's in his late forties or early fifties, with salt-and-pepper hair. The suit he's wearing is the kind I aspire to be able to afford. Everything about him screams wealth, including the eye-poppingly expensive watch on his left wrist.

"Hi." Enya greets him with a smile. I don't bother saying anything since I figure it's her he's interested in talking to.

"Great performance," he says, flashing perfectly straight, white teeth.

"Thank you."

He offers her his hand. "I'm William Samson. It's a pleasure to meet you."

Samson? The same one who owns the sportswear

company? My eyes bug out, and when I glance at Enya, hers have done the same.

"It's lovely to meet you too, Mr. Samson," she says, shaking his hand.

"William, please." He turns his gaze to me. "I'm so glad I caught you before you left. I got away from the meet and greet for a while, but I have to be back soon. I hope you don't mind me turning up here."

"Not at all." Although I don't understand why he came.

"It's not often that an athlete passes up an opportunity like the one we gave you today, let alone for the reasons you did." He nods toward Enya. "Samson & Sons Sportswear are a family company. We value loyalty, and we like to endorse athletes who share our values." His smile widens. "You showed very clearly that you do." He reaches into his pocket and withdraws a business card. "This is my direct phone number and address. We're hosting a lunch tomorrow for the athletes we're most impressed with. I'd like you to come."

I take the card with trembling hands, hardly able to believe what I'm hearing. Surely there's been some kind of mistake. "Tomorrow?" I ask in case I've misunderstood.

"At 1:00 p.m.," he confirms. "You're welcome to bring Enya and Brian."

"Thank you." It slowly dawns on me that this is actually happening. A massive, career-changing sponsor is chasing me. He left his own company event to track me down and personally invite me to lunch. I shake my head, feeling dizzy with the insanity of it all. "Thank you so much. We'll be there."

"Glad to hear it." He pats me on the shoulder. "I

have to get back. Enjoy your night." With that, he turns and is swallowed up by the crowd.

"Oh my God." Enya plants a kiss on my cheek. "You're in!"

"I can't believe he came here."

"Of course he did. You're awesome and he knows it." Movement to the side captures her attention. Her parents are waving at her. She catches my eyes for a moment, communicating without words, and then walks toward them.

Seth appears in the place where William Samson had been standing. "Was that the son part of Samson & Sons Sportswear?"

"He's interested in sponsoring me," I whisper. "*Me.*"

He claps me on the shoulder. "That's great, Jimmy. He couldn't have chosen a better guy."

Disbelief has me gaping. He really thinks that? He and I haven't always gotten along perfectly, and I respect the hell out of the guy, but I'm not always sure where I stand with him. "That means a lot." I laugh. "Brian is going to wet himself with excitement."

The rest of the people from the gym gather around us, along with Enya's extended, slightly nutty family. We stay in the arena for a while, then make our way back to Enya's place. I park on the road outside the house and get out of the car, but Enya stops me before I go inside. She draws me around the corner, out of sight of the others. I peer down at her face in the dim lighting. Her eyes shine with happiness. As always, her beauty hits me like a gut punch.

"Sorry, I wanted a moment to ourselves," she says quietly.

"I like having you to myself." I kiss the tip of her nose. For once, I'm completely at peace. The constant voice of doubt in my mind has shut up. I know with every part of my heart I'm where I'm supposed to be, and I'm no longer so scared of everything being torn away from me. Enya is with me, whatever may come. And I'm with her. "You might not know this, but you've given me a reason to be happy. You're everything to me, Enya. I want to share life with you from here on out."

She wraps her arms around me and rests her cheek over my heart. It's thundering louder and faster than usual, and she must be able to hear it. "You've helped give me faith in myself again." She speaks softly, but I can hear every word. "You're the kind of man I always wanted but thought I'd never have. Thank you for being you. I will happily share my life with you. I'll give you all my tomorrows—if you give me yours."

"That sounds pretty fucking perfect to me."

EPILOGUE

Tempe

I make my way through the throng of people in the bar near the arena. The event's *official* after-party—which I chose to attend rather than Enya's personal one, because it serves my purpose better—has gotten out of control. It's what I need, though. I've spent the past few days crying my eyes out, and I'm sick of it. I'm not the type to wallow, which means I have to move the hell on.

I scan the men jammed into the room. Many of them wear apparel from martial arts gyms, and several others I've seen before. They won't do. I need a stranger. Not just any stranger, but one gorgeous enough to drive Chad from my mind for a few hours. I'm wiping the slate clean. I check out a guy leaning against the wall, chatting to a couple I don't know. He's tall, built, but doesn't have the wow factor I'm looking for. There's a hot blond who could be an option, but as I watch, his arm goes around a cute redhead.

Then I see him.

I know instinctively he's the one I want. Nobody else can compare. The man is alone in the corner, sipping beer. He's jaw-droppingly good-looking, with tousled black hair and a chiseled jaw. But what really catches my attention are the colorful tattoos that twist up his muscled forearms and disappear beneath the rolled-up sleeves of his shirt. They're exquisite, and they emphasize how very different he is from Chad, who believes in button-downs for any occasion and would burst a blood vessel before letting a tattooist anywhere near him. I'd always appreciated his clean-cut good looks, but he's pretty uptight. This guy, on the other hand.…

He's anything but.

I run a hand over my braided hair, relieved I wore a slinky dress to the fights tonight. In my usual apparel of MMA shorts and a baggy tank top, Mr. Tattoos wouldn't give me a second look, but in this, he might. Gathering my courage—and a glass of wine—I make my way over to him. He's focused intently on his phone and doesn't look up as I approach.

"You look like you could use some company." I hope I don't sound as awkward as I feel. I haven't been on the dating scene for a couple of years, and my flirting skills are rusty.

"No, I—" His eyes flick to mine. They're the most unusual shade of blue, like a watercolor sky. He cuts off halfway through what I suspect was going to be a brush-off. He straightens and pockets his phone. An easy smile slides across his face, and my lady parts chorus "Hallelujah." He's even more beautiful when he smiles. "That depends on what the company is offering."

I bite my lower lip. I'm not sure if I can do this. The man is every bit as delicious as he looked from a distance. Could someone like him really be interested in a one-night stand with someone like me?

Guess there's only one way to find out.

"No names, no personal details, no strings." I hold my breath, waiting for his response.

To my absolute astonishment, he cups my face between two tattooed hands and brushes his mouth over mine. That soft touch sends a wave of desire pooling between my legs. His lips are fuller than I thought, and he tastes faintly of beer, but not in an unpleasant way.

"Okay, Miss Mystery," he murmurs as he pulls back, capturing me with a soulful gaze that sees more than I'd like. "I'm all yours."

EXTENDED EPILOGUE – TWO MONTHS LATER

Jimmy

I land a solid cross to my opponent's jaw and dance out of the way before he strikes back. He's taller than me and has a longer reach, so I have to get into the pocket of space immediately surrounding him if I want to do any damage. Fighting someone with longer limbs is challenging, but not impossible. Mostly, it requires nerves of fucking steel.

I throw a jab, then duck low and deliver a body punch, pivoting out of the way as he tries to block me. He clips my shoulder with a glancing blow, but I barely notice. Adrenaline is fueling me. I'm so close to winning I can practically smell it. There's a roar in the background. Our fight has been a bloodbath, and the crowd loves it. My opponent snaps his shin into my thigh before I have time to check it, and I wince as my leg wobbles. The guy has a killer kick and he's been using it over and over again. I'm going to need a fuckton of ice and several days of rest after this. I test how well my injured leg holds my weight. It's managing all right, but I'm not sure it will for much longer.

My opponent lands a hook that only my quick reflexes block from hitting my right temple. He follows it up with a cross. I see my opportunity. While the guard on his right side is down, I snap my foot in an arc and slam it into the side of his head. He drops. The crowd screams. The referee hurries to his side and counts the seconds, then he indicates it's over. I've won via knockout. Fuck yeah.

A pair of medics hurry into the cage to check over my opponent, who is slowly coming around. I hover nearby until he's gotten to his feet and has an arm slung around one of the medic's shoulders.

"That was a crazy fight." I nod respectfully. "You really did some damage, man."

He nods, although his eyes are a little unfocused. "Great kick."

The medics steer him away, and I return to my corner. Seth scans me and then tousles my hair, as though he's afraid he'll hurt me if he touches me anywhere else. I laugh, but it cuts short because of a sharp pain in my ribs.

"You killed it out there," Seth says. "Go get your medal, then the medics will want to see you too."

"You got it, boss." I head back to the referee and stand alone in the middle of the cage, where I'm presented with a medal for winning. The announcer calls my name over the speakers, and I raise a fist in triumph. I don't do anything too showy, though. Not when it was such a good scrap, and I honestly hope the other guy is okay. I'm escorted out of the cage by one of the medics and I sit on a bench out the back while she examines me.

"You've probably got bruised ribs," she says, as

though that isn't obvious with the massive shadow growing along my side. "But I see no evidence they're broken." She sighs. "You're going to be black and blue for quite some time. Stay off your feet as much as possible and take it easy. No training this week. Got it?"

"Yes, ma'am."

She narrows her eyes and turns to Enya and Seth, who are standing beside me. "You'll keep him in line?"

Enya nods firmly. "Don't worry. I'll take good care of him."

"Good." She stands. "Listen to your girlfriend."

"You did awesome out there," Enya exclaims as soon as she's gone. "What a battle."

Seth hums his agreement. "You made us all proud. Now go home and rest up. I'll come by to debrief tomorrow."

"Okay. See you then."

Seth offers a fist for me to bump, then strides away, leaving me alone with Enya.

She caresses my one unblemished cheekbone. "I hate seeing you hurt."

"Back at you." I wince because every inch of my body seems to be battered. "Part of the job, though."

"I know." She sits beside me. "But I fully intend to run around after you for the next few days." She touches her lips softly to my forehead, then draws back and smiles mischievously. "I'm hoping you'll make it easier for me."

"Oh yeah?" I tilt my head back and study the planes of her beautiful face. "How?"

"By moving in with me."

My heart pounds against my rib cage. Did I hear that right? "Holy fuck, are you serious?"

Her grin widens. "Deadly. You've practically been living with me anyway. Why not make it official?"

"I'd love that." Despite my aches and pains, a sense of warmth and contentment flows through me. "You're amazing, Enya Sears, and I love you."

She kisses my cheek, my neck, my shoulder. "I love you more than anything." She twines her fingers through mine. "Come on, let's get you home."

I wobble to my feet, and she wraps an arm around my waist to support me. My leg is already stiffening up, and I can tell it's going to be nearly impossible to walk tomorrow.

"By the way," she adds. "My family are coming to visit. They meant to surprise you by being here for the fight, but their plane got delayed. I hope you don't mind, but they'll all be turning up tonight."

I close my eyes, and my throat thickens. God, I love that nutty family. "Sounds perfect. I can't wait." Tired and sore or not, it's true. Because with Enya and her family, I have everything I've longed for all my life. She makes me grateful to be me, and in return, I show her every day how special she is. We've become one of those nauseatingly adorable couples, and I wouldn't have it any other way.

THE END

FIGHTER'S MERCY EXCERPT

Mercy

I roll my suitcase across the asphalt driveway toward a building that looks like it came straight from the Italian countryside. Pale orange walls, a reddish roof, and behind it are grapevines as far as the eye can see. It's idyllic. The perfect setting for my best friend Isiah's wedding. And hopefully a good place for me to forget about the growing stack of unpaid bills on the counter at home. I cringe at the thought of the letter that arrived this morning, reminding me of the costs owing for Danny's funeral. Insult to injury, considering the medical bills related to trying to keep him alive are what got me into financial trouble in the first place. But I'll pay. Somehow. Meanwhile, during my time in Napa Valley, I intend to do my best to forget.

I check in at the front counter and the receptionist hands me a set of keys. Isiah booked accommodation for the entire bridal party in the lead-up to the wedding. I'm halfway along the corridor when I hear a voice that stops me in my tracks. I strain my ears, trying to hear it again.

"...so glad there's air conditioning," the disembodied female voice continues. "It's hot out there."

My jaw drops.

It can't be.

But I swear the woman sounds just like my Miss Mystery—who gave me the most incredible night of my life and then vanished. I'd hoped our hours together might lead to something more. She'd been gorgeous, with just a hint of vulnerability that intrigued me. She'd said one night only, but I thought I'd have the chance to talk her around. Except she left before dawn. Out of respect for her wishes, I didn't try to find her. But now, it seems, the universe has handed me a golden opportunity.

I follow the sound of voices—someone else is speaking now—around a corner and into a small communal area where a pair of sofas face each other. On the far side, Hazel, Isiah's bride-to-be, is seated beside a pale brunette, her best friend. Seated opposite, with her back to me, is a woman in a black tank top, with an elegantly sloped neck and toned shoulders. A memory flashes into my mind of me lowering my mouth to the curve of her neck and sucking on her rich, brown skin until she shivered.

"Hey, Mercy." Hazel gets to her feet and comes around to hug me. I smile but I can't take my eyes off her companion. "Did you have a good trip?"

"It was a nice drive," I reply on autopilot. Miss Mystery is starting to turn, but I can't tell if she recognizes me.

"I think you've met my maid of honor, Karen," Hazel says.

The brunette waggles her fingers in a flirty wave. I nod to her.

"And this is my childhood best friend, Tempe. She's the bridesmaid."

Tempe.

I finally have a name to go with the face and body that have been haunting my dreams.

Tempe's deep brown eyes lock on mine and she stiffens. Oh yeah, she recognizes me.

"You," she breathes. "Oh my God."

That's when she stands up and I see what I couldn't before.

She's pregnant.

Her belly is rounded enough that there's no doubting it. The air seizes in my lungs. Based on the size of the bump, she's five or six months along, which means she either moved on from me quickly or was already pregnant when we were together. Neither option is something I want to dwell on.

"Congratulations." I force myself to smile. "You look great."

Her jaw firms and she rounds the sofa and grabs my arm. "Excuse me," she says to her friends. "We'll be back soon."

She tugs me away from them. I barely have the presence of mind to drag my suitcase behind us. I follow her around several corners, not processing where we're going. My mind is too busy protesting the unfairness of finally seeing her again when I apparently won't have a chance to pursue anything with her. She stops in a small alcove beside the ladies' room. I find myself scanning her fingers for a ring, but don't see one.

"Here's the thing." Her words are choked, and I get the feeling she's barely holding herself together, although I'm not sure why. She's clearly moved on, so what would make her so upset about running into an old fling? Sure, it's awkward under the circumstances, but it's hardly enough to warrant the expression of dread that's twisting her features. "Shit, this is hard."

"What is it?" I ask, hoping I sound encouraging. If she's trying to gently let me know we won't be having a repeat, I kinda figured as much the second I laid eyes on her baby bump.

She clears her throat and looks me straight in the eye. "You're the father of my baby."

ALSO BY A. RIVERS

Crown MMA Romance: The Outsiders

Fighter's Frenemy

Fighter's Fake Out

Fighter's Mercy

Fighter's Forever

Crown MMA Romance

Fighter's Heart

Fighter's Best Friend

Fighter's Secret

Fighter's Second Chance

King's Security

The King

The Veteran

ACKNOWLEDGMENTS

Thank you, first and foremost, to my husband, who has helped me accomplish so many of my dreams and stood by me whenever I've needed it. Thank you to Kate and Donna for helping make this book the best it could be, and to Maria at Steamy Designs for the awesome cover design. Thank you to my author friends, and to the other wonderful folks in the publishing industry. Lastly, thank you to my friends and family for your ongoing support. You mean the world to me.

ABOUT THE AUTHOR

Alexa (A.) Rivers writes romance with strong heroes and heroines who kick butt and take names. She loves MMA fighters, investigators, military men, body-guards, and the protective guy next door who isn't afraid to fight the odds for love. She also writes small town romance as Alexa Rivers.